Short Stories

THEODORE DREISER

DOVER PUBLICATIONS, INC.
New York

DOVER THRIFT EDITIONS
GENERAL EDITOR: STANLEY APPELBAUM
EDITOR OF THIS VOLUME: CANDACE WARD

Copyright

Copyright © 1994 by Dover Publications, Inc.
All rights reserved under Pan American and International Copyright Conventions.

Published in Canada by General Publishing Company, Ltd., 30 Lesmill Road, Don Mills, Toronto, Ontario.
Published in the United Kingdom by Constable and Company, Ltd., 3 The Lanchesters, 162–164 Fulham Palace Road, London W6 9ER.

Bibliographical Note

This Dover edition, first published in 1994, is a new selection of short stories, reprinted unabridged from *Free and Other Stories*, published by Boni and Liveright, Inc., New York, in 1918. An introductory note has been specially prepared for this edition.

Library of Congress Cataloging-in-Publication Data

Dreiser, Theodore, 1871–1945.
   [Free, and other stories. Selections]
   Short stories / Theodore Dreiser.
      p.   cm. — (Dover thrift editions)
   A selection of stories from: Free, and other stories.
   ISBN 0-486-28215-5 (pbk.)
   I. Title.   II. Series.
PS3507.R55A6   1994
813'.52 — dc20
                                 94-7857
                                    CIP

Manufactured in the United States of America
Dover Publications, Inc., 31 East 2nd Street, Mineola, N.Y. 11501

Note

THEODORE DREISER (1871–1945) was one of ten children, the son of a stern German Catholic father and a sympathetic mother. At a very early age Dreiser experienced severe poverty; his childhood was punctuated by frequent moves throughout the Midwest as his family searched for work and adequate housing. Such early hardships so impressed Dreiser that a keen sense of social oppression and injustice informs all his writing.

Dreiser began his literary career — after a year at the University of Indiana, subsidized by a former high school teacher — as a journalist, working for newspapers in Chicago, St. Louis, Pittsburgh and finally New York. In 1894 he began writing magazine articles, and in 1900 one of his most famous novels, *Sister Carrie*, was published. The novel came under attack for immorality — its "sinful" heroine goes unpunished for her transgressions — and sold only 456 copies. Other writers, however, such as Frank Norris, H. G. Wells and Sherwood Anderson, praised Dreiser's work for its unflinching naturalism. By the time Dreiser published *Free and Other Stories* in 1918, such naturalism was more acceptable to the American public, and Dreiser's ability to portray a range of human emotions with compassion and dignity was better appreciated. In the five stories included here, Dreiser pits his characters against social forces that stifle and oppress. In "Free" a man realizes, on the eve of his wife's death, the depth of his sacrifices for the sake of convention. In "The Second Choice" a young working-class woman is faced with the drab and inevitable reality of her future. In "Nigger Jeff" a young reporter witnesses the lynching of a black man. Though Dreiser's portrayal of the lynched man may appear offensive to modern readers, his depiction of the tragedy reveals his insight into human motivations, for good and bad. Together these stories represent Dreiser's commitment to realism, to what Sherwood Anderson described as "greater courage and fidelity to life in writing."

Contents

Introduction by Sherwood Anderson   ix

Free   1

Nigger Jeff   29

The Lost Phœbe   51

The Second Choice   65

Married   83

Introduction[1]

THEODORE DREISER is a man who, with the passage of time, is bound to loom larger and larger in the awakening æsthetic consciousness of America. Among all of our prose writers he is one of the few men of whom it may be said that he has always been an honest workman, always impersonal, never a trickster. Read this book of Dreiser's, *Free and Other Stories*, and then compare it with a book of short stories, say by Bret Harte or O. Henry. The tradition of trick writing began early among us in America and has flowered here like some strange fungus growth. Every one knows there are no plot short stories in life itself and yet the tradition of American short story writing has been built almost entirely upon the plot idea. Human nature, the strange little whims, tragedies and comedies of life itself, have everywhere been sacrificed to the need of plot and one reads the ordinary plot story of the magazines with a kind of growing wonder. "Is there no comedy, no tragedy, no irony in life itself? If it is there why do not our writers find it out and set it forth? Why these everlasting falsehoods, this ever-present bag of tricks?"

One is sometimes convinced, in thinking of the matter, that, among most of our prose writers, there is left no feeling at all for life, and the prose writer, at least the tale teller, who has no feeling for life is no artist. There is the man or woman who walks beside me in the street, works beside me in the office, sits beside me in the theatre. What has happened in the lives of all these people? Why do our writers so determinedly spend all their time inventing people who never had any existence — puppets — these impossible cowboys, detectives, society adventurers? Are most of our successful short story writers too lazy to find out something about life itself, the occasional flashes of wonder and

---

1. This introduction appears in the 1918 Modern Library edition by Boni and Liveright, Inc., New York.

strangeness in life? It is apparent they are. Either they are too lazy or they are afraid of life, tremble before it.

But Theodore Dreiser is not afraid. He does not tremble. Often I have thought of him as the bravest man who has lived in America in our times. Perhaps I exaggerate. He is a man of my own craft and always he has been a heroic figure in my own eyes. He is honest. Never in any line he has ever written will you find him resorting to the trick to get himself out of a hard situation. The beauty and the ironic terror of life is like a wall before him but he faces the wall. He does not mutter cheap little lies in the darkness and to me there is something honorable and fine in the fact that in him there is no lack of courage in facing his materials, that he needs resort to tricks of style to cover.

Dreiser is a middle-westerner, large of frame, rather shy, brusque in manner and in his person singularly free from the common small vanities of the artist class. I often wonder if he knows how much he is loved and respected for what he has done by hundreds of unknown writers everywhere, fellows just trying to get ground under their feet. If there is a modern movement in American prose writing, a movement toward greater courage and fidelity to life in writing, then Theodore Dreiser is the pioneer and the hero of the movement. Of that I think there can be no question. I think it is true now that no American prose writer need hesitate before the task of putting his hands upon his materials. Puritanism, as a choking, smothering force, is dead or dying. We are rapidly approaching the old French standard wherein the only immorality for the artist is in bad art and I think that Theodore Dreiser, the man, has done more than any living American to bring this about. All honor to him. The whole air of America is sweeter to breathe because he had lived and worked here. He has laid a foundation upon which any sort of structure may be built. It will stand the strain. His work has been honestly and finely done. The man has laid so many old ghosts, pounded his way through such a wall of stupid prejudices and fears that today any man coming into the craft of writing comes with a new inheritance of freedom.

In the middle-western country in which Dreiser grew to manhood there could have been no awareness of the artist's obligations. How his own feet found the path they have followed so consistently I do not know. One gets so little from his own writings, from those little flashes by which every artist reveals himself in his work, that helps toward an understanding of his fine courage. Grey smoky hurried towns, Terre Haute, Indiana, Chicago, St. Louis, and the other places wherein he worked and lived, a life of hard work for small pay in dreary places. Twain had at least the rough and tumble heartiness of western life, the romance of the old Mississippi river days, and as for the eastern men who came before Dreiser, the Hawthornes, Emersons (and one is compelled to include the Howellses) they grew out of a European culture, were the children of a European culture, a fact that no doubt advantaged them while it has been of so little help to the Americans who are seeking masters to aid them in finding a life and a basis for a culture of their own.

Our earlier New England writers knew Europe and Europe knew them and accepted them as distant cousins anyway, but in Terre Haute, Indiana, in Dreiser's day there, when his own life was forming — if any of his fellow countrymen of that day and place ever crossed the sea I dare say they went to the Holy Land and came back with a bottle of Jordan Water. The only knowledge they had of the work and the aims of European artists was got from reading that most vulgar of all our Mark Twain's books, *The Innocents Abroad.* The idea of an artist, with all of the strange tangle of dreams and hopes in his brain being also a workman, owing something to his craft and to the materials of his craft, would have been as strange to the Terre Haute or the St. Louis of twenty-five years ago as a camel sitting and smoking a pipe on the court-house steps.

And it was out of such a grey blankness (from the artist's point of view, at least) that the man Dreiser came and he came alone, making his own path. What a figure he has made of himself, always pounding at the wall of stupidity before him, throwing aside always the cheap triumph to be got by trickery, always giving himself fully and honestly to the life about him, trying to understand it, never lying to himself or to others. One thinks of such a life and is appalled.

There is that story we have all heard of the young Dostoevsky, when he had written his first book, *Poor Folks.* He gave the manuscript to a writer friend who took it home and read it and in the middle of the night drove to the home of a publisher, filled with excitement. The two men sat up together and read the manuscript aloud and then, although it was four in the morning drove through the wintry streets to the young writer's lodgings. There was joy, excitement, happy fellow craftsmen, even tears of joy. A new and great writer had come into Russian life. What glad recognition. It was like a wedding or a birth. Men were happy together and you may imagine how the young craftsman felt.

That happened in Russia and in America Dreiser wrote his *Sister Carrie* and it was published and later buried out of sight in the cellar of a publishing house, for some ten years I believe, and might have been there yet but for the fighting impulses of our critics, our Hacketts, Menckens and Dells. Some woman, a relative perhaps of some member of the publishing firm, had decided the book was immoral and today one reads with wonder, seeking in vain for the immorality and only made glad by its sympathetic understanding of life.

Theodore Dreiser, whose book *Free and Other Stories* is now included in the famous Modern Library series, has lived out most of his life as a comparatively poor man. He might have grown rich had he but joined the ranks of the clever tricksters or had he devoted his energies to turning out romantic sentimentalities. What amusing and clever men we have had in his time, what funny fellows, what masters of all the tricks of writing.

Where are they? What have they given us?

And what has Dreiser given us? A fine growing and glowing tradition, has he not, a new sense of the value of our own lives, a new interest in the life about us, in offices, streets and houses.

Theodore Dreiser's nature is the true artist's nature, so little understood among us. He is no reformer. In his work, as in the man himself, there is something bold, with all the health of true boldness, and at the same time something very finely humble. He stands before life, looking at it, trying to understand it that he may catch its significance and its drama. He is not always crying, "Look at me! See what I am doing!" He is the workman, full of self-respect, and — most strange and wonderful of all for an American writer — full of respect for his materials, for the lives of those who come close to him, for that world of people who have come into life under his pen.

As for my trying to make in any detailed way an estimate of the value of the man's work, that is beyond me. The man has done, is doing, his job, he has fought his way through darkness into the light and in making a pathway for himself he has made a pathway for us all. Because he had lived and worked so honestly and finely America is a better place for all workmen. As for his work, there it stands — sturdy, strong, true and fine and most of all free from all the many cheap tricks of our craft.

And as for the man himself, there he also stands. One knows Dreiser will never stoop to tricky, second rate work; cannot, being Dreiser, ever so stoop. He is, however, not given to advertising himself. He stays in the background and lets the work speak for the man. It is the kind of fine, honest work that is coming to mean more and more every year to a growing army of sincere American craftsmen.

SHERWOOD ANDERSON

Free[1]

THE LARGE and rather comfortable apartment of Rufus Haymaker, architect, in Central Park West, was very silent. It was scarcely dawn yet, and at the edge of the park, over the way, looking out from the front windows which graced this abode and gave it its charm, a stately line of poplars was still shrouded in a gray morning mist. From his bedroom at one end of the hall, where, also, a glimpse of the park was to be had, came Mr. Haymaker at this early hour to sit by one of these broader windows and contemplate these trees and a small lake beyond. He was very fond of Nature in its manifold art forms — quite poetic, in fact.

He was a tall and spare man of about sixty, not ungraceful, though slightly stoop-shouldered, with heavy overhanging eyebrows and hair, and a short, professionally cut gray mustache and beard, which gave him a severe and yet agreeable presence. For the present he was clad in a light-blue dressing gown with silver cords, which enveloped him completely. He had thin, pale, long-fingered hands, wrinkled at the back and slightly knotted at the joints, which bespoke the artist, in mood at least, and his eyes had a weary and yet restless look in them.

For only yesterday Doctor Storm, the family physician, who was in attendance on his wife, ill now for these three weeks past with a combination of heart lesion, kidney poisoning and neuritis, had taken him aside and said very softly and affectionately, as though he were trying to spare his feelings: "To-morrow, Mr. Haymaker, if your wife is no better I will call in my friend, Doctor Grainger, whom you know, for a consultation. He is more of an expert in these matters of the heart" — the heart, Mr. Haymaker had time to note ironically — "than I am. Together we will make a thorough examination, and then I hope we will be better able to say what the possibilities of her recovery really are. It's been a very trying case, a very stubborn one, I might say. Still, she has a great deal of vitality and is doing as well as could be expected, all things considered.

---

1. "Free" first appeared in *The Saturday Evening Post*, March 16, 1918.

At the same time, though I don't wish to alarm you unnecessarily — and there is no occasion for great alarm yet — still I feel it my duty to warn you that her condition is very serious indeed. Not that I wish you to feel that she is certain to die. I don't think she is. Not at all. Just the contrary. She may get well, and probably will, and live all of twenty years more." (Mentally Mr. Haymaker sighed a purely spiritual sigh.) "She has fine recuperative powers, so far as I can judge, but she has a bad heart, and this kidney trouble has not helped it any. Just now, when her heart should have the least strain, it has the most.

"She is just at that point where, as I may say, things are in the balance. A day or two, or three or four at the most, ought to show which way things will go. But, as I have said before, I do not wish to alarm you unnecessarily. We are not nearly at the end of our tether. We haven't tried blood transfusion yet, and there are several arrows to that bow. Besides, at any moment she may respond more vigorously to medication than she has heretofore — especially in connection with her kidneys. In that case the situation would be greatly relieved at once.

"However, as I say, I feel it my duty to speak to you in this way in order that you may be mentally prepared for any event, because in such an odd combination as this the worst may happen at any time. We never can tell. As an old friend of yours and Mrs. Haymaker's, and knowing how much you two mean to each other" — Mr. Haymaker merely stared at him vacantly — "I feel it my duty to prepare you in this way. We all of us have to face these things. Only last year I lost my dear Matilda, my youngest child, as you know. Just the same, as I say, I have the feeling that Mrs. Haymaker is not really likely to die soon, and that we — Doctor Grainger and myself — will still be able to pull her through. I really do."

Doctor Storm looked at Mr. Haymaker as though he were very sorry for him — an old man long accustomed to his wife's ways and likely to be made very unhappy by her untimely end; whereas Mr. Haymaker, though staring in an almost sculptural way, was really thinking what a farce it all was, what a dull mixture of error and illusion on the part of all. Here he was, sixty years of age, weary of all this, of life really — a man who had never been really happy in all the time that he had been married; and yet here was his wife, who from conventional reasons believed that he was or should be, and who on account of this was serenely happy herself, or nearly so. And this doctor, who imagined that he was old and weak and therefore in need of this loving woman's care and sympathy and understanding! Unconsciously he raised a deprecating hand.

Also his children, who thought him dependent on her and happy with her; his servants and her and his friends thinking the same thing, and yet he really was not. It was all a lie. He was unhappy. Always he had been unhappy, it seemed, ever since he had been married — for over thirty-one years now. Never in all that time, for even so much as a single day, had he ever done anything but long, long, long, in a pale, constrained way — for what, he scarcely dared think — not to be married any more — to be free — to be as he was before ever he saw Mrs. Haymaker.

And yet being conventional in mood and training and utterly domesticated by time and conditions over which he seemed not to have much control — nature, custom, public opinion, and the like, coming into play as forces — he had drifted, had not taken any drastic action. No, he had merely drifted, wondering if time, accident or something might not interfere and straighten out his life for him, but it never had. Now weary, old, or rapidly becoming so, he condemned himself for his inaction. Why hadn't he done something about it years before? Why hadn't he broken it up before it was too late, and saved his own soul, his longing for life, color? But no, he had not. Why complain so bitterly now?

All the time the doctor had talked this day before he had wanted to smile a wry, dry, cynical smile, for in reality he did not want Mrs. Haymaker to live — or at least at the moment he thought so. He was too miserably tired of it all. And so now, after nearly twenty-four hours of the same unhappy thought, sitting by this window looking at a not distant building which shone faintly in the haze, he ran his fingers through his hair as he gazed, and sighed.

How often in these weary months, and even years, past — ever since he and his wife had been living here, and before — had he come to these or similar windows while she was still asleep, to sit and dream! For some years now they had not even roomed together, so indifferent had the whole state become; though she did not seem to consider that significant, either. Life had become more or less of a practical problem to her, one of position, place, prestige. And yet how often, viewing his life in retrospect, had he wished that his life had been as sweet as his dreams — that his dreams had come true.

After a time on this early morning, for it was still gray, with the faintest touch of pink in the east, he shook his head solemnly and sadly, then rose and returned along the hall to his wife's bedroom, at the door of which he paused to look where she lay seriously ill, and beside her in an armchair, fast asleep, a trained nurse who was supposedly keeping the night vigil ordered by the doctor, but who no doubt was now very weary. His wife was sleeping also — very pale, very thin now, and very weak. He felt sorry for her at times, in spite of his own weariness; now, for instance. Why need he have made so great a mistake so long ago? Perhaps it was his own fault for not having been wiser in his youth. Then he went quietly on to his own room, to lie down and think.

Always these days, now that she was so very ill and the problem of her living was so very acute, the creeping dawn thus roused him — to think. It seemed as though he could not really sleep soundly any more, so stirred and distrait was he. He was not so much tired or physically worn as mentally bored or disappointed. Life had treated him so badly, he kept thinking to himself over and over. He had never had the woman he really wanted, though he had been married so long, had been faithful, respectable and loved by her, in her way. "In her way," he half quoted to himself as he lay there.

Presently he would get up, dress and go down to his office as usual if his wife were not worse. But — but, he asked himself — would she be? Would that slim and yet so durable organism of hers — quite as old as his own, or nearly so — break under the strain of this really severe illness? That would set him free again, and nicely, without blame or comment on him. He could then go where he chose once more, do as he pleased — think of that — without let or hindrance. For she was ill at last, so very ill, the first and really great illness she had endured since their marriage. For weeks now she had been lying so, hovering, as it were, between life and death, one day better, the next day worse, and yet not dying, and with no certainty that she would, and yet not getting better either. Doctor Storm insisted that it was a leak in her heart which had suddenly manifested itself which was causing all the real trouble. He was apparently greatly troubled as to how to control it.

During all this period Mr. Haymaker had been, as usual, most sympathetic. His manner toward her was always soft, kindly, apparently tender. He had never really begrudged her anything — nothing certainly that he could afford. He was always glad to see her and the children humanly happy — though they, too, largely on account of her, he thought, had proved a disappointment to him — because he had always sympathized with her somewhat unhappy youth, narrow and stinted; and yet he had never been happy himself, either, never in all the time that he had been married. If she had endured much, he kept telling himself when he was most unhappy, so had he, only it was harder perhaps for women to endure things than men — he was always willing to admit that — only also she had had his love, or thought she had, an actual spiritual peace, which he had never had. She knew she had a faithful husband. He felt that he had never really had a wife at all, not one that he could love as he knew a wife should be loved. His dreams as to that!

Going to his office later this same day — it was in one of those tall buildings that face Madison Square — he had looked first, in passing, at the trees that line Central Park West, and then at the bright wall of apartment houses facing it, and meditated sadly, heavily. Here the sidewalks were crowded with nursemaids and children at play, and in between them, of course, the occasional citizen loitering or going about his errands. The day was so fine, so youthful, as spring days will seem at times. As he looked, especially at the children, and the young men bustling office-ward, mostly in new spring suits, he sighed and wished that he were young once more. Think how brisk and hopeful they were! Everything was before them. They could still pick and choose — no age or established conditions to stay them. Were any of them, he asked himself for the thousandth time, it seemed to him, as wearily connected as he had been at their age? Did they each have a charming young wife to love — one of whom they were passionately fond — such a one as he had never had; or did they not?

Wondering, he reached his office on one of the topmost floors of one of those highest buildings commanding a wide view of the city, and surveyed it wearily. Here were visible the two great rivers of the city, its towers and spires and far-flung walls. From these sometimes, even yet, he seemed to gain a patience to live, to hope. How in his youth all this had inspired him — or that other city that was then. Even now he was always at peace here, so much more so than in his own home, pleasant as it was. Here he could look out over this great scene and dream or he could lose the memory in his work that his love-life had been a failure. The great city, the buildings he could plan or supervise, the efficient help that always surrounded him — his help, not hers — aided to take his mind off himself and that deep-seated inner ache or loss.

The care of Mr. Haymaker's apartment during his wife's illness and his present absence throughout the day, devolved upon a middle-aged woman of great seriousness, Mrs. Elfridge by name, whom Mrs. Haymaker had employed years before; and under her a maid of all work, Hester, who waited on table, opened the door, and the like; and also at present two trained nurses, one for night and one for day service, who were in charge of Mrs. Haymaker. The nurses were both bright, healthy, blue-eyed girls, who attracted Mr. Haymaker and suggested all the youth he had never had — without really disturbing his poise. It would seem as though that could never be any more.

In addition, of course, there was the loving interest of his son Wesley and his daughter Ethelberta — whom his wife had named so in spite of him — both of whom had long since married and had children of their own and were living in different parts of the great city. In this crisis both of them came daily to learn how things were, and occasionally to stay for the entire afternoon or evening, or both. Ethelberta had wanted to come and take charge of the apartment entirely during her mother's illness, only Mrs. Haymaker, who was still able to direct, and fond of doing so, would not hear of it. She was not so ill but that she could still speak, and in this way could inquire and direct. Besides, Mrs. Elfridge was as good as Mrs. Haymaker in all things that related to Mr. Haymaker's physical comfort, or so she thought.

If the truth will come out — as it will in so many pathetic cases — it was never his physical so much as his spiritual or affectional comfort that Mr. Haymaker craved. As said before, he had never loved Mrs. Haymaker, or certainly not since that now long-distant period back in Muskegon, Michigan, where both had been born and where they had lived and met at the ages, she of fifteen, he of seventeen. It had been, strange as it might seem now, a love match at first sight with them. She had seemed so sweet, a girl of his own age or a little younger, the daughter of a local chemist. Later, when he had been forced by poverty to go out into the world to make his own way, he had written her much, and imagined her to be all that she had seemed at fifteen, and more — a dream among fair women. But Fortune, slow in coming to his aid and fickle in fulfilling his dreams, had brought it about that for several years more he had been compelled to stay away nearly all of the time, unable to marry her; during which period, unknown to himself really, his own point of view had altered. How it had happened he could never tell really, but so it was. The great city, larger experiences — while she was still enduring the smaller ones — other faces, dreams of larger things, had all combined to destroy it or her, only he had not quite realized it then. He was always so slow in realizing the full import of the immediate thing, he thought.

That was the time, as he had afterward told himself — how often! — that he should have discovered his mistake and stopped. Later it always seemed to become more and more impossible. Then, in spite of some heartache to her and some distress to himself, no doubt, all would be well for him now. But no; he had been too inexperienced, too ignorant, too bound by all the conventions and punctilio of his simple Western world. He thought an engagement, however unsatisfactory it might come to seem afterward, was an engagement, and binding. An honorable man would not break one — or so his country moralists argued.

Yes, at that time he might have written her, he might have told her, then. But he had been too sensitive and kindly to speak of it. Afterward it was too late. He feared to wound her, to undo her, to undo her life. But now — now — look at his! He had gone back on several occasions before marriage, and might have seen and done and been free if he had had but courage and wisdom — but no; duty, order, the beliefs of the region in which he had been reared, and of America — what it expected and what she expected and was entitled to — had done for him completely. He had not spoken. Instead, he had gone on and married her without speaking of the change in himself, without letting her know how worse than ashes it had all become. God, what a fool he had been! how often since he had told himself over and over.

Well, having made a mistake it was his duty perhaps, at least according to current beliefs, to stick by it and make the best of it; — a bargain was a bargain in marriage, if no where else — but still that had never prevented him from being unhappy. He could not prevent that himself. During all these long years, therefore, owing to these same conventions — what people would think and say — he had been compelled to live with her, to cherish her, to pretend to be happy with her — "another perfect union," as he sometimes said to himself. In reality he had been unhappy, horribly so. Even her face wearied him at times, and her presence, her mannerisms. Only this other morning Doctor Storm, by his manner indicating that he thought him lonely, in danger of being left all alone and desperately sad and neglected in case she died had irritated him greatly. Who would take care of him? his eyes had seemed to say — and yet he himself wanted nothing so much as to be alone for a time, at least, in this life, to think for himself, to do for himself, to forget this long, dreary period in which he had pretended to be something that he was not.

Was he never to be rid of the dull round of it, he asked himself now, never before he himself died? And yet shortly afterward he would reproach himself for these very thoughts, as being wrong, hard, unkind — thoughts that would certainly condemn him in the eyes of the general public, that public which made reputations and one's general standing before the world.

During all this time he had never even let her know — no, not once — of the tremendous and soul-crushing sacrifice he had made. Like the Spartan boy, he had concealed the fox gnawing at his vitals. He had not complained. He had been, indeed, the model husband, as such things go in conventional walks. If you doubted it look at his position, or that of his children; or his wife — her mental and physical comfort, even in her illness, her unfailing belief that he was all he should be! Never once apparently, during all these years, had she doubted his love or felt him to be unduly unhappy — or, if not that exactly, if not fully accepting his love as something that was still at a fever heat, the thing it once was — still believing that he found pleasure and happiness in being with her, a part of the home which together they had built up, these children they had reared, comfort in knowing that it would endure to the end! To the end! During all these years she had gone on molding his and her lives — as much as that was possible in his case — and those of their children, to suit herself; and thinking all the time that she was doing what he wanted or at least what was best for him and them.

How she adored convention! What did she not think she knew in regard to how things ought to be — mainly what her old home surroundings had taught her, the American idea of this, that and the other. Her theories in regard to friends, education of the children, and so on, had in the main prevailed, even when he did not quite agree with her; her desires for certain types of pleasure and amusement, of companionship, and so on, were conventional types always and had also prevailed. There had been little quarrels, of course, always had been — what happy home is free of them? — but still he had always given in, or nearly always, and had acted as though he were satisfied in so doing.

But why, therefore, should he complain now, or she ever imagine, or ever have imagined, that he was unhappy? She did not, had not. Like all their relatives and friends of the region from which they sprang, and here also — and she had been most careful to regulate that, courting whom she pleased and ignoring all others — she still believed most firmly, more so than ever, that she knew what was best for him, what he really thought and wanted. It made him smile most wearily at times.

For in her eyes — in regard to him, at least, not always so with others, he had found — marriage was a sacrament, sacrosanct, never to be dissolved. One life, one love. Once a man had accepted the yoke or even asked a girl to marry him it was his duty to abide by it. To break an engagement, to be unfaithful to a wife, even unkind to her — what a crime, in her eyes! Such people ought to be drummed out of the world. They were really not fit to live — dogs, brutes!

And yet, look at himself — what of him? What of one who had made a mistake in regard to all this? Where was his compensation to come from, his peace and happiness? Here on earth or only in some mythical heaven — that odd, angelic heaven that she still believed in? What a farce! And all her friends and his would think he would be so miserable now if she died, or at least ought to be. So far had asinine convention and belief in custom carried the world. Think of it!

But even that was not the worst. No; that was not the worst, either. It had been the gradual realization coming along through the years that he had married an essentially small, narrow woman who could never really grasp his point of view — or, rather, the significance of his dreams or emotions — and yet with whom, nevertheless, because of this original promise or mistake, he was compelled to live. Grant her every quality of goodness, energy, industry, intent — as he did freely — still there was this;

and it could never be adjusted, never. Essentially, as he had long since discovered, she was narrow, ultraconventional, whereas he was an artist by nature, brooding and dreaming strange dreams and thinking of far-off things which she did not or could not understand or did not sympathize with, save in a general and very remote way. The nuances of his craft, the wonders and subtleties of forms and angles — had she ever realized how significant these were to him, let alone to herself? No, never. She had not the least true appreciation of them — never had had. Architecture? Art? What could they really mean to her, desire as she might to appreciate them? And he could not now go elsewhere to discover that sympathy. No. He had never really wanted to, since the public and she would object, and he thinking it half evil himself.

Still, how was it, he often asked himself, that Nature could thus allow one conditioned or equipped with emotions and seekings such as his, not of an utterly conventional order, to seek out and pursue one like Ernestine, who was not fitted to understand him or to care what his personal moods might be? Was love truly blind, as the old saw insisted, or did Nature really plan, and cleverly, to torture the artist mind — as it did the pearl-bearing oyster with a grain of sand — with something seemingly inimical, in order that it might produce beauty? Sometimes he thought so. Perhaps the many interesting and beautiful buildings he had planned — the world called them so, at least — had been due to the loving care he lavished on them, being shut out from love and beauty elsewhere. Cruel Nature, that cared so little for the dreams of man — the individual man or woman!

At the time he had married Ernestine he was really too young to know exactly what it was he wanted to do or how it was he was going to feel in the years to come; and yet there was no one to guide him, to stop him. The custom of the time was all in favor of this dread disaster. Nature herself seemed to desire it — mere children being the be-all and the end-all of everything everywhere. Think of that as a theory! Later, when it became so clear to him what he had done, and in spite of all the conventional thoughts and conditions that seemed to bind him to this fixed condition, he had grown restless and weary, but never really irritable. No, he had never become that.

Instead he had concealed it all from her, persistently, in all kindness; only this hankering after beauty of mind and body in ways not represented by her had hurt so — grown finally almost too painful to bear. He had dreamed and dreamed of something different until it had become almost an obsession. Was it never to be, that something different, never, anywhere, in all time? What a tragedy! Soon he would be dead and then it would never be anywhere — anymore! Ernestine was charming, he would admit, or had been at first, though time had proved that she was not charming to him either mentally or physically in any compelling way; but how did that help him now? How could it? He had actually found himself bored by her for more than twenty-seven years now, and this other dream growing, growing, growing—until——

But now he was old; and she was dying, or might be, and it could not make so much difference what happened to him or to her; only it could, too, because he wanted to be free for a little while, just for a little while, before he died.

To be free! free!

One of the things that had always irritated him about Mrs. Haymaker was this, that in spite of his determination never to offend the social code in any way—he had felt for so many reasons, emotional as well as practical, that he could not afford so to do—and also in spite of the fact that he had been tortured by this show of beauty in the eyes and bodies of others, his wife, fearing perhaps in some strange psychic way that he might change, had always tried to make him feel or believe— premeditatedly and of a purpose, he thought—that he was not the kind of man who would be attractive to women; that he lacked some physical fitness, some charm that other men had, which would cause all young and really charming women to turn away from him. Think of it! He to whom so many women had turned with questioning eyes!

Also that she had married him largely because she had felt sorry for him! He chose to let her believe that, because he was sorry for her. Because other women had seemed to draw near to him at times in some appealing or seductive way she had insisted that he was not even a cavalier, let alone a Lothario; that he was ungainly, slow, uninter-esting—to all women but her!

Persistently, he thought, and without any real need, she had harped on this, fighting chimeras, a chance danger in the future; though he had never given her any real reason, and had never even planned to sin against her in any way—never. She had thus tried to poison his own mind in regard to himself and his art—and yet—and yet—— Ah, those eyes of other women, their haunting beauty, the flitting something they said to him of infinite, inexpressible delight. Why had his life been so very hard?

One of the disturbing things about all this was the iron truth which it had driven home, namely, that Nature, unless it were expressed or represented by some fierce determination within, which drove one to do, be, cared no whit for him or any other man or woman. Unless one acted for oneself, upon some stern conclusion nurtured within, one might rot and die spiritually. Nature did not care. "Blessed be the meek" — yes. Blessed be the strong, rather, for they made their own happiness. All these years in which he had dwelt and worked in this knowledge, hoping for something but not acting, nothing had happened, except to him, and that in an unsatisfactory way. All along he had seen what was happening to him; and yet held by convention he had refused to act always, because somehow he was not hard enough to act. He was not strong enough, that was the real truth — had not been. Almost like a bird in a cage, an animal peeping out from behind bars, he had viewed the world of free thought and freer action. In many a drawing-room, on the street, or in his own home even, had he not looked into an eye, the face of someone who seemed to offer understanding, to know, to sympathize, though she might not have, of course; and yet religiously and moralistically, like an anchorite, because of duty and current belief and what people would say and think, Ernestine's position and faith in him, her comfort, his career and that of the children — he had put them all aside, out of his mind, forgotten them almost, as best he might. It had been hard at times, and sad, but so it had been.

And look at him now, old, not exactly feeble yet — no, not that yet, not quite! — but life weary and almost indifferent. All these years he had wanted, wanted — wanted — an understanding mind, a tender heart, the some one woman — she must exist somewhere — who would have sympathized with all the delicate shades and meanings of his own character, his art, his spiritual as well as his material dreams —— And yet look at him! Mrs. Haymaker had always been with him, present in the flesh or the spirit, and — so ——

Though he could not ever say that she was disagreeable to him in a material way — he could not say that she had ever been that exactly — still she did not correspond to his idea of what he needed, and so —— Form had meant so much to him, color; the glorious perfectness of a glorious woman's body, for instance, the color of her thoughts, moods — exquisite they must be, like his own at times; but no, he had never had the opportunity to know one intimately. No, not one, though he had dreamed of her so long. He had never even dared whisper this to any one, scarcely to himself. It was not wise, not socially fit. Thoughts like this would tend to social ostracism in his circle, or rather hers — for had she not made the circle?

And here was the rub with Mr. Haymaker, at least, that he could not make up his mind whether in his restlessness and private mental complaints he were not even now guilty of a great moral crime in so thinking. Was it not true that men and women should be faithful in marriage whether they were happy or not? Was there not some psychic law governing this matter of union — one life, one love — which made the thoughts and the pains and the subsequent sufferings and hardships of the individual, whatever they might be, seem unimportant? The churches said so. Public opinion and the law seemed to accept this. There were so many problems, so much order to be disrupted, so much pain caused, many insoluble problems where children were concerned — if people did not stick. Was it not best, more blessed — socially, morally, and in every other way important — for him to stand by a bad bargain rather than to cause so much disorder and pain, even though he lost his own soul emotionally? He had thought so — or at least he had acted as though he thought so — and yet —— How often had he wondered over this!

Take, now, some other phases. Granting first that Mrs. Haymaker had, according to the current code, measured up to the requirements of a wife, good and true, and that at first after marriage there had been just enough of physical and social charm about her to keep his state from becoming intolerable, still there was this old ache; and then newer things which came with the birth of the several children: First Elwell — named after a cousin of hers, not his — who had died only two years after he was born; and then Wesley; and then Ethelberta. How he had always disliked that name! — largely because he had hoped to call her Ottilie, a favorite name of his; or Janet, after his mother.

Curiously the arrival of these children and the death of poor little Elwell at two had somehow, in spite of his unrest, bound him to this matrimonial state and filled him with a sense of duty, and pleasure even — almost entirely apart from her, he was sorry to say — in these young lives; though if there had not been children, as he sometimes told himself, he surely would have broken away from her; he could not have stood it. They were so odd in their infancy, those little ones, so troublesome and yet so amusing — little Elwell, for instance, whose nose used to crinkle with delight when he would pretend to bite his neck, and whose gurgle of pleasure was so sweet and heart-filling that it positively thrilled and lured him. In spite of his thoughts concerning Ernestine — and always in those days they were rigidly put down as unmoral and even evil, a certain unsocial streak in him perhaps which was against law and order and social well-being — he came to have a deep and abiding feeling for Elwell. The latter, in some chemic, almost unconscious way, seemed to have arrived as a balm to his misery, a bandage for his growing wound — sent by whom, by what, how? Elwell had seized upon his imagination, and so his heartstrings — had come, indeed, to make him feel understanding and sympathy there in that little child; to supply, or seem to at least, what he lacked in the way of love and affection from one whom he could truly love. Elwell was never so happy apparently as when snuggling in his arms, not Ernestine's, or lying against his neck. And when he went for a walk or elsewhere there was Elwell always ready, arms up, to cling to his neck. He seemed, strangely enough, inordinately fond of his father, rather than his mother, and never happy without him. On his part, Haymaker came to be wildly fond of him — that queer little lump of a face, suggesting a little of himself and of his own mother, not so much of Ernestine, or so he thought, though he would not have objected to that. Not at all. He was not so small as that. Toward the end of the second year, when Elwell was just beginning to be able to utter a word or two, he had taught him that silly old rhyme which ran "There were three kittens," and when it came to "and they shall have no —— " he would stop and say to Elwell, "What now?" and the latter would gurgle "puh!" — meaning, of course, pie.

Ah, those happy days with little Elwell, those walks with him over his shoulder or on his arm, those hours in which of an evening he would rock him to sleep in his arms! Always Ernestine was there, and happy in the thought of his love for little Elwell and her, her more than anything else perhaps; but it was an illusion — that latter part. He did not care for her even then as she thought he did. All his fondness was for Elwell, only she took it as evidence of his growing or enduring affection for her — another evidence of the peculiar working of her mind. Women were like that, he supposed — some women.

And then came that dreadful fever, due to some invading microbe which the doctors could not diagnose or isolate, infantile paralysis perhaps; and little Elwell had finally ceased to be as flesh and was eventually carried forth to the lorn, disagreeable graveyard near Wood-lawn. How he had groaned internally, indulged in sad, despondent thoughts concerning the futility of all things human, when this had happened! It seemed for the time being as if all color and beauty had really gone out of his life for good.

"Man born of woman is of few days and full of troubles," the preacher whom Mrs. Haymaker had insisted upon having into the house at the time of the funeral had read. "He fleeth also as a shadow and continueth not."

Yes; so little Elwell had fled, as a shadow, and in his own deep sorrow at the time he had come to feel the first and only sad, deep sympathy for Ernestine that he had ever felt since marriage; and that because she had suffered so much — had lain in his arms after the funeral and cried so bitterly. It was terrible, her sorrow. Terrible — a mother grieving for her first-born! Why was it, he had thought at the time, that he had never been able to think or make her all she ought to be to him? Ernestine at this time had seemed better, softer, kinder, wiser, sweeter than she had ever seemed; more worthy, more interesting than ever he had thought her before. She had slaved so during the child's illness, stayed awake night after night, watched over him with such loving care — done everything, in short, that a loving human heart could do to rescue her young from the depths; and yet even then he had not really been able to love her. No, sad and unkind as it might seem, he had not. He had just pitied her and thought her better, worthier! What cursed stars disordered the minds and moods of people so? Why was it that these virtues of people, their good qualities, did not make you love them, did not really bind them to you, as against the things you could not like? Why? He had resolved to do better in his thoughts, but somehow, in spite of himself, he had never been able so to do.

Nevertheless, at that time he seemed to realize more keenly than ever her order, industry, frugality, a sense of beauty within limits, a certain laudable ambition to do something and be somebody — only, only he could not sympathize with her ambitions, could not see that she had anything but a hopelessly common-place and always unimportant point of view. There was never any flare to her, never any true distinction of mind or soul. She seemed always, in spite of anything he might say or do, hopelessly to identify doing and being with money and current opinion — neighborhood public opinion, almost — and local social position, whereas he knew that distinguished doing might as well be connected with poverty and shame and disgrace as with these other things — wealth and station, for instance; a thing which she could never quite understand apparently, though he often tried to tell her, much against her mood always.

Look at the cases of the great artists! Some of the greatest architects right here in the city, or in history, were of peculiar, almost disagreeable, history. But no, Mrs. Haymaker could not understand anything like that, anything connected with history, indeed — she hardly believed in history, its dark, sad pages, and would never read it, or at least did not care to. And as for art and artists — she would never have believed that wisdom and art understanding and true distinction might take their rise out of things necessarily low and evil — never.

Take now, the case of young Zingara. Zingara was an architect like himself, whom he had met more than thirty years before, here in New York, when he had first arrived, a young man struggling to become an architect of significance, only he was very poor and rather unkempt and disreputable-looking. Haymaker had found him several years before his marriage to Ernestine in the dark offices of Pyne & Starboard, Architects, and had been drawn to him definitely; but because he smoked all the time and was shabby as to his clothes and had no money — why, Mrs. Haymaker, after he had married her, and though he had known Zingara nearly four years, would have none of him. To her he was low, and a failure, one who would never succeed. Once she had seen him in some cheap restaurant that she chanced to be passing, in company with a drabby-looking maid, and that was the end.

"I wish you wouldn't bring him here any more, dear," she had insisted; and to have peace he had complied — only, now look. Zingara had since become a great architect, but now of course, owing to Mrs. Haymaker, he was definitely alienated. He was the man who had since designed the Æsculapian Club; and Symphony Hall with its delicate façade; as well as the tower of the Wells Building, sending its sweet lines so high, like a poetic thought or dream. But Zingara was now a dreamy recluse like himself, very exclusive, as Haymaker had long since come to know, and indifferent as to what people thought or said.

But perhaps it was not just obtuseness to certain of the finer shades and meanings of life, but an irritating aggressiveness at times, backed only by her limited understanding, which caused her to seek and wish to be here, there and the other place; wherever, in her mind, the truly successful — which meant nearly always the materially successful of a second or third rate character — were, which irritated him most of all. How often had he tried to point out the difference between true and shoddy distinction — the former rarely connected with great wealth.

But no. So often she seemed to imagine such queer people to be truly successful, when they were really not — usually people with just money, or a very little more.

And in the matter of rearing and educating and marrying their two children, Wesley and Ethelberta, who had come after Elwell — what peculiar pains and feelings had not been involved in all this for him. In infancy both of these had seemed sweet enough, and so close to him, though never quite so wonderful as Elwell. But, as they grew, it seemed somehow as though Ernestine had come between him and them. First, it was the way she had raised them, the very stiff and formal manner in which they were supposed to move and be, copied from the few new-rich whom she had chanced to meet through him — and admired in spite of his warnings. That was the irony of architecture as a profession — it was always bringing such queer people close to one, and for the sake of one's profession, sometimes, particularly in the case of the young architect, one had to be nice to them. Later, it was the kind of school they should attend. He had half imagined at first that it would be the public school, because they both had begun as simple people; but no, since they were prospering it had to be a private school for each, and not one of his selection, either — or hers, really — but one to which the Barlows and the Westervelts, two families of means with whom Ernestine had become intimate, sent their children and therefore thought excellent!

The Barlows! Wealthy, but, to him, gross and mediocre people who had made a great deal of money in the manufacture of patent medicines out West, and who had then come to New York to splurge, and had been attracted to Ernestine — not him particularly, he imagined — because Haymaker had built a town house for them, and also because he was gaining a fine reputation. They were dreadful really, so *gauche*, so truly dull; and yet somehow they seemed to suit Ernestine's sense of fitness and worth at the time, because, as she said, they were good and kind — like her Western home folks; only they were not really. She just imagined so. They were worthy enough people in their way, though with no taste. Young Fred Barlow had been sent to the expensive Gaillard School for Boys, near Morristown, where they were taught manners and airs, and little else, as Haymaker always thought, though Ernestine insisted that they were given a religious training as well. And so Wesley had to go there — for a time, anyhow. It was the best school.

And similarly, because Mercedes Westervelt, senseless, vain little thing, was sent to Briarcliff School, near White Plains, Ethelberta had to go there. Think of it! It was all so silly, so pushing. How well he remembered the long, delicate campaign which preceded this, the logic and tactics employed, the importance of it socially to Ethelberta, the tears and cajolery. Mrs. Haymaker could always cry so easily, or seem to be on the verge of it, when she wanted anything; and somehow, in spite of the fact that he knew her tears were unimportant, or timed and for a purpose, he could never stand out against them, and she knew it. Always he felt moved or weakened in spite of himself. He had no weapon wherewith to fight them, though he resented them as a part of the argument. Positively Mrs. Haymaker could be as sly and as ruthless as Machiavelli himself at times, and yet believe all the while that she was tender, loving, self-sacrificing, generous, moral and a dozen other things, all of which led to the final achievement of her own aims. Perhaps this was admirable from one point of view, but it irritated him always. But if one were unable to see him- or herself, their actual disturbing inconsistencies, what were you to do?

And again, he had by then been married so long that it was almost impossible to think of throwing her over, or so it seemed at the time. They had reached the place then where they had supposedly achieved position together, though in reality it was all his — and not such position as he was entitled to, at that. Ernestine — and he was thinking this in all kindness—could never attract the ideal sort. And anyhow, the mere breath of a scandal between them, separation or unfaithfulness, which he never really contemplated, would have led to endless bickering and social and commercial injury, or so he thought. All her strong friends— and his, in a way—those who had originally been his clients, would have deserted him. Their wives, their own social fears, would have compelled them to ostracize him! He would have been a scandal-marked architect, a brute for objecting to so kind and faithful and loving a wife. And perhaps he would have been, at that. He could never quite tell, it was all so mixed and tangled.

Take, again, the marriage of his son Wesley into the De Gaud family—George de Gaud *père* being nothing more than a retired real-estate speculator and promoter who had money, but nothing more; and Irma de Gaud, the daughter, being a gross, coarse, sensuous girl, physically attractive no doubt, and financially reasonably secure, or so she had seemed; but what else? Nothing, literally nothing; and his son had seemed to have at least some spiritual ideals at first. Ernestine had taken up with Mrs. George de Gaud—a miserable, narrow creature, so Hay-maker thought—largely for Wesley's sake, he presumed. Anyhow, every-thing had been done to encourage Wesley in his suit and Irma in her toleration, and now look at them! De Gaud *père* had since failed and left his daughter practically nothing. Irma had been interested in anything but Wesley's career, had followed what she considered the smart among the new-rich—a smarter, wilder, newer new-rich than ever Ernestine had fancied, or could. To-day she was without a thought for anything besides teas and country clubs and theaters—and what else?

And long since Wesley had begun to realize it himself. He was an engineer now, in the employ of one of the great construction com-panies, a moderately successful man. But even Ernestine, who had engineered the match and thought it wonderful, was now down on her. She had begun to see through her some years ago, when Irma had begun to ignore her; only before it was always the De Gauds here, and the De Gauds there. Good gracious, what more could any one want than the De Gauds—Irma de Gaud, for instance? Then came the concealed dissension between Irma and Wesley, and now Mrs. Hay-maker insisted that Irma had held, and was holding Wesley back. She was not the right woman for him. Almost—against all her prejudices— she was willing that he should leave her. Only, if Haymaker had broached anything like that in connection with himself!

And yet Mrs. Haymaker had been determined, because of what she considered the position of the De Gauds at that time, that Wesley should marry Irma. Wesley now had to slave at mediocre tasks in order to have enough to allow Irma to run in so-called fast society of a second or third rate. And even at that she was not faithful to him — or so Haymaker believed. There were so many strange evidences. And yet Haymaker felt that he did not care to interfere now. How could he? Irma was tired of Wesley, and that was all there was to it. She was looking elsewhere, he was sure.

Take but one more case, that of Ethelberta. What a name! In spite of all Ernestine's determination to make her so successful and thereby reflect some credit on her had she really succeeded in so doing? To be sure, Ethelberta's marriage was somewhat more successful financially than Wesley's had proved to be, but was she any better placed in other ways? John Kelso — "Jack," as she always called him — with his light ways and lighter mind, was he really any one! — anything more than a waster? His parents stood by him no doubt, but that was all; and so much the worse for him. According to Mrs. Haymaker at the time, he, too, was an ideal boy, admirable, just the man for Ethelberta, because the Kelsos, *père* and *mère*, had money. Horner Kelso had made a kind of fortune in Chicago in the banknote business, and had settled in New York, about the time that Ethelberta was fifteen, to spend it. Ethelberta had met Grace Kelso at school.

And now see! She was not unattractive, and had some pleasant, albeit highly affected, social ways; she had money, and a comfortable apartment in Park Avenue; but what had it all come to? John Kelso had never done anything really, nothing. His parents' money and indulgence and his early training for a better social state had ruined him if he had ever had a mind that amounted to anything. He was idle, pleasure-loving, mentally indolent, like Irma de Gaud. Those two should have met and married, only they could never have endured each other. But how Mrs. Haymaker had courted the Kelsos in her eager and yet diplomatic way, giving teas and receptions and theater parties; and yet he had never been able to exchange ten significant words with either of them, or the younger Kelsos either. Think of it!

And somehow in the process Ethelberta, for all his early affection and tenderness and his still kindly feeling for her, had been weaned away from him and had proved a limited and conventional girl, somewhat like her mother, and more inclined to listen to her than to him — though he had not minded that really. It had been the same with Wesley before her. Perhaps, however, a child was entitled to its likes and dislikes, regardless.

But why had he stood for it all, he now kept asking himself. Why? What grand results, if any, had been achieved? Were their children so wonderful? — their lives? Would he not have been better off without her — his children better, even, by a different woman? — hers by a different man? Wouldn't it have been better if he had destroyed it all, broken away? There would have been pain, of course, terrible consequences, but even so he would have been free to go, to do, to reorganize his life on another basis. Zingara had avoided marriage entirely — wise man. But no, no; always convention, that long list of reasons and terrors he was always reciting to himself. He had allowed himself to be pulled round by the nose, God only knows why, and that was all there was to it. Weakness, if you will, perhaps; fear of convention; fear of what people would think and say.

Always now he found himself brooding over the dire results to him of all this respect on his part for convention, moral order, the duty of keeping society on an even keel, of not bringing disgrace to his children and himself and her, and yet ruining his own life emotionally by so doing. To be respectable had been so important that it had resulted in spiritual failure for him. But now all that was over with him, and Mrs. Haymaker was ill, near to death, and he was expected to wish her to get well, and be happy with her for a long time yet! Be happy! In spite of anything he might wish or think he ought to do, he couldn't. He couldn't even wish her to get well.

It was too much to ask. There was actually a haunting satisfaction in the thought that she might die now. It wouldn't be much, but it would be something — a few years of freedom. That was something. He was not utterly old yet, and he might have a few years of peace and comfort to himself still — and — and —— That dream — that dream — though it might never come true now — it couldn't really — still — still —— He wanted to be free to go his own way once more, to do as he pleased, to walk, to think, to brood over what he had not had — to brood over what he had not had! Only, only, whenever he looked into her pale sick face and felt her damp limp hands he could not quite wish that, either; not quite, not even now. It seemed too hard, too brutal — only — only —— So he wavered.

No; in spite of her long-past struggle over foolish things and in spite of himself and all he had endured or thought he had, he was still willing that she should live; only he couldn't wish it exactly. Yes, let her live if she could. What matter to him now whether she lived or died? Whenever he looked at her he could not help thinking how helpless she would be without him, what a failure at her age, and so on. And all along, as he wryly repeated to himself, she had been thinking and feeling that she was doing the very best for him and her and the children! — that she was really the ideal wife for him, making every dollar go as far as it would, every enjoyment yield the last drop for them all, every move seeming to have been made to their general advantage! Yes, that was true. There was a pathos about it, wasn't there? But as for the actual results——!

The next morning, the second after his talk with Doctor Storm, found him sitting once more beside his front window in the early dawn, and so much of all this, and much more, was coming back to him, as before. For the thousandth or the ten-thousandth time, as it seemed to him, in all the years that had gone, he was concluding again that his life was a failure. If only he were free for a little while just to be alone and think, perhaps to discover what life might bring him yet; only on this occasion his thoughts were colored by a new turn in the situation. Yesterday afternoon, because Mrs. Haymaker's condition had grown worse, the consultation between Grainger and Storm was held, and to-day some-time transfusion was to be tried, that last grim stand taken by physicians in distress over a case; blood taken from a strong ex-cavalryman out of a position, in this case, and the best to be hoped for, but not assured. In this instance his thoughts were as before wavering. Now supposing she really died, in spite of this? What would he think of himself then? He went back after a time and looked in on her where she was still sleeping. Now she was not so strong as before, or so she seemed; her pulse was not so good, the nurse said. And now as before his mood changed in her favor, but only for a little while. For later, waking, she seemed to look and feel better.

Later he came up to the dining room, where the nurse was taking her breakfast, and seating himself beside her, as was his custom these days, asked: "How do you think she is to-day?"

He and the night nurse had thus had their breakfasts together for days. This nurse, Miss Filson, was such a smooth, pink, graceful creature, with light hair and blue eyes, the kind of eyes and color that of late, and in earlier years, had suggested to him the love time or youth that he had missed.

The latter looked grave, as though she really feared the worst but was concealing it.

"No worse, I think, and possibly a little better," she replied, eying him sympathetically. He could see that she too felt that he was old and in danger of being neglected. "Her pulse is a little stronger, nearly normal now, and she is resting easily. Doctor Storm and Doctor Grainger are coming, though, at ten. Then they'll decide what's to be done. I think if she's worse that they are going to try transfusion. The man has been engaged. Doctor Storm said that when she woke to-day she was to be given strong beef tea. Mrs. Elfridge is making it now. The fact that she is not much worse, though, is a good sign in itself, I think."

Haymaker merely stared at her from under his heavy gray eyebrows.

He was so tired and gloomy, not only because he had not slept much of late himself but because of this sawing to and fro between his varying moods. Was he never to be able to decide for himself what he really wished? Was he never to be done with this interminable moral or spiritual problem? Why could he not make up his mind on the side of moral order, sympathy, and be at peace? Miss Filson pattered on about other heart cases, how so many people lived years and years after they were supposed to die of heart lesion; and he meditated as to the grayness and strangeness of it all, the worthlessness of his own life, the variability of his own moods. Why was he so? How queer — how almost evil, sinister — he had become at times; how weak at others. Last night as he had looked at Ernestine lying in bed, and this morning before he had seen her, he had thought if she only would die — if he were only really free once more, even at this late date. But then when he had seen her again this morning and now when Miss Filson spoke of transfusion, he felt sorry again. What good would it do him now? Why should he want to kill her? Could such evil ideas go unpunished either in this world or the next? Supposing his children could guess! Supposing she did die now — and he wished it so fervently only this morning — how would he feel? After all, Ernestine had not been so bad. She had tried, hadn't she? — only she had not been able to make a success of things, as he saw it, and he had not been able to love her, that was all. He reproached himself once more now with the hardness and the cruelty of his thoughts.

The opinion of the two physicians was that Mrs. Haymaker was not much better and that this first form of blood transfusion must be resorted to — injected straight via a pump — which should restore her greatly provided her heart did not bleed it out too freely. Before doing so, however, both men once more spoke to Haymaker, who in an excess of self-condemnation insisted that no expense must be spared. If her life was in danger, save it by any means — all. It was precious to her, to him and to her children. So he spoke. Thus he felt that he was lending every force which could be expected of him, aside from fervently wishing for her recovery, which even now, in spite of himself, he could not do. He was too weary of it all, the conventional round of duties and obligations. But if she recovered, as her physicians seemed to think she might if transfusion were tried, if she gained even, it would mean that he would have to take her away for the summer to some quiet mountain resort — to be with her hourly during the long period in which she would be recovering. Well, he would not complain now. That was all right. He would do it. He would be bored of course, as usual, but it would be too bad to have her die when she could be saved. Yes, that was true. And yet ——

He went down to his office again and in the meantime this first form of transfusion was tried, and proved a great success, apparently. She was much better, so the day nurse phoned at three; very much better. At five-thirty Mr. Haymaker returned, no unsatisfactory word having come in the interim, and there she was, resting on a raised pillow, if you please, and looking so cheerful, more like her old self than he had seen her in some time.

At once then his mood changed again. They were amazing, these variations in his own thoughts, almost chemic, not volitional, decidedly peculiar for a man who was supposed to know his own mind — only did one, ever? Now she would not die. Now the whole thing would go on as before. He was sure of it. Well, he might as well resign himself to the old sense of failure. He would never be free now. Everything would go on as before, the next and the next day the same. Terrible! Though he seemed glad — really grateful, in a way, seeing her cheerful and hopeful once more — still the obsession of failure and being once more bound forever returned now. In his own bed at midnight he said to himself: "Now she will really get well. All will be as before. I will never be free. I will never have a day — a day! Never!"

But the next morning, to his surprise and fear or comfort, as his moods varied, she was worse again; and then once more he reproached himself for his black thoughts. Was he not really killing her by what he thought? he asked himself — these constant changes in his mood? Did not his dark wishes have power? Was he not as good as a murderer in his way? Think, if he had always to feel from now on that he had killed her by wishing so! Would not that be dreadful — an awful thing really? Why was he this way? Could he not be human, kind?

When Doctor Storm came at nine-thirty, after a telephone call from the nurse, and looked grave and spoke of horses' blood as being better, thicker than human blood — not so easily bled out of the heart when injected as a serum — Haymaker was beside himself with self-reproaches and sad, disturbing fear. His dark, evil thoughts of last night and all these days had done this, he was sure. Was he really a murderer at heart, a dark criminal, plotting her death? — and for what? Why had he wished last night that she would die? Her case must be very desperate.

"You must do your best," he now said to Doctor Storm. "Whatever is needful — she must not die if you can help it."

"No, Mr. Haymaker," returned the latter sympathetically. "All that can be done will be done. You need not fear. I have an idea that we didn't inject enough yesterday, and anyhow human blood is not thick enough in this case. She responded, but not enough. We will see what we can do to-day."

Haymaker, pressed with duties, went away, subdued and sad. Now once more he decided that he must not tolerate these dark ideas any more, must rid himself of these black wishes, whatever he might feel. It was evil. They would eventually come back to him in some dark way, he might be sure. They might be influencing her. She must be allowed to recover if she could without any opposition on his part. He must now make a further sacrifice of his own life, whatever it cost. It was only decent, only human. Why should he complain now, anyhow, after all these years! What difference would a few more years make? He returned at evening, consoled by his own good thoughts and a telephone message at three to the effect that his wife was much better. This second injection had proved much more effective. Horses' blood was plainly better for her. She was stronger, and sitting up again. He entered at five, and found her lying there pale and weak, but still with a better light in her eye, a touch of color in her cheeks — or so he thought — more force, and a very faint smile for him, so marked had been the change. How great and kind Doctor Storm really was! How resourceful! If she would only get well now! If this dread siege would only abate! Doctor Storm was coming again at eight.

"Well, how are you, dear?" she asked, looking at him sweetly and lovingly, and taking his hand in hers.

He bent and kissed her forehead — a Judas kiss, he had thought up to now, but not so to-night. To-night he was kind, generous — anxious, even, for her to live.

"All right, dearest; very good indeed. And how are you? It's such a fine evening out. You ought to get well soon so as to enjoy these spring days."

"I'm going to," she replied softly. "I feel so much better. And how have you been? Has your work gone all right?"

He nodded and smiled and told her bits of news. Ethelberta had phoned that she was coming, bringing violets. Wesley had said he would be here at six, with Irma! Such-and-such people had asked after her. How could he have been so evil, he now asked himself, as to wish her to die? She was not so bad — really quite charming in her way, an ideal wife for some one, if not him. She was as much entitled to live and enjoy her life as he was to enjoy his; and after all she was the mother of his children, had been with him all these years. Besides, the day had been so fine — it was now — a wondrous May evening. The air and sky were simply delicious. A lavender haze was in the air. The telephone bell now ringing brought still another of a long series of inquiries as to her condition. There had been so many of these during the last few days, the maid said, and especially to-day — and she gave Mr. Haymaker a list of names. See, he thought, she had even more friends than he, being so good, faithful, worthy. Why should he wish her ill?

He sat down to dinner with Ethelberta and Wesley when they arrived, and chatted quite gayly — more hopefully than he had in weeks. His own varying thoughts no longer depressing him, for the moment he was happy. How were they? What were the children all doing? At eight-thirty Doctor Storm came again, and announced that he thought Mrs. Haymaker was doing very well indeed, all things considered.

"Her condition is fairly promising, I must say," he said. "If she gets through another night or two comfortably without falling back I think she'll do very well from now on. Her strength seems to be increasing a fraction. However, we must not be too optimistic. Cases of this kind are very treacherous. To-morrow we'll see how she feels, whether she needs any more blood."

He went away, and at ten Ethelberta and Wesley left for the night, asking to be called if she grew worse, thus leaving him alone once more. He sat and meditated. At eleven, after a few moments at his wife's bedside — absolute quiet had been the doctor's instructions these many days — he himself went to bed. He was very tired. His varying thoughts had afflicted him so much that he was always tired, it seemed — his evil conscience, he called it — but to-night he was sure he would sleep. He felt better about himself, about life. He had done better, to-day. He should never have tolerated such dark thoughts. And yet — and yet — and yet——

He lay on his bed near a window which commanded a view of a small angle of the park, and looked out. There were the spring trees, as usual, silvered now by the light, a bit of lake showing at one end. Here in the city a bit of sylvan scenery such as this was so rare and so expensive. In his youth he had been so fond of water, any small lake or stream or pond. In his youth, also, he had loved the moon, and to walk in the dark. It had all, always, been so suggestive of love and happiness, and he had so craved love and happiness and never had it. Once he had designed a yacht club, the base of which suggested waves. Once, years ago, he had thought of designing a lovely cottage or country house for himself and some new love — that wonderful one — if ever she came and he were free. How wonderful it would all have been. Now — now — the thought at such an hour and especially when it was too late, seemed sacrilegious, hard, cold, unmoral, evil. He turned his face away from the moonlight and sighed, deciding to sleep and shut out these older and darker and sweeter thoughts if he could, and did.

Presently he dreamed, and it was as if some lovely spirit of beauty — that wondrous thing he had always been seeking — came and took him by the hand and led him out, out by dimpling streams and clear rippling lakes and a great, noble highway where were temples and towers and figures in white marble. And it seemed as he walked as if something had been, or were, promised him — a lovely fruition to something which he craved — only the world toward which he walked was still dark or shadowy, with something sad and repressing about it, a haunting sense of a still darker distance. He was going toward beauty apparently, but he was still seeking, seeking, and it was dark there when —

"Mr. Haymaker! Mr. Haymaker!" came a voice — soft, almost mystical at first, and then clearer and more disturbing, as a hand was laid on him. "Will you come at once? It's Mrs. Haymaker!"

On the instant he was on his feet seizing the blue silk dressing gown hanging at his bed's head, and adjusting it as he hurried. Mrs. Elfridge and the nurse were behind him, very pale and distrait, wringing their hands. He could tell by that that the worst was at hand. When he reached the bedroom — her bedroom — there she lay as in life — still, peaceful, already limp, as though she were sleeping. Her thin, and as he sometimes thought, cold, lips were now parted in a faint, gracious smile, or trace of one. He had seen her look that way, too, at times; a really gracious smile, and wise, wiser than she was. The long, thin, graceful hands were open, the fingers spread slightly apart as though she were tired, very tired. The eyelids, too, rested wearily on tired eyes. Her form, spare as always, was outlined clearly under the thin coverlets. Miss Filson, the night nurse, was saying something about having fallen asleep for a moment, and waking only to find her so. She was terribly depressed and disturbed, possibly because of Doctor Storm.

Haymaker paused, greatly shocked and moved by the sight — more so than by anything since the death of little Elwell. After all, she had tried, according to her light. But now she was dead — and they had been together so long! He came forward, tears of sympathy springing to his eyes, then sank down beside the bed on his knees so as not to disturb her right hand where it lay.

"Ernie, dear," he said gently, "Ernie — are you really gone?" His voice was full of sorrow; but to himself it sounded false, traitorous.

He lifted the hand and put it to his lips sadly, then leaned his head against her, thinking of his long, mixed thoughts these many days, while both Mrs. Elfridge and the nurse began wiping their eyes. They were so sorry for him, he was so old now!

After a while he got up — they came forward to persuade him at last — looking tremendously sad and distrait, and asked Mrs. Elfridge and the nurse not to disturb his children. They could not aid her now. Let them rest until morning. Then he went back to his own room and sat down on the bed for a moment, gazing out on the same silvery scene that had attracted him before. It was dreadful. So then his dark wishing had come true at last? Possibly his black thoughts had killed her after all. Was that possible? Had his voiceless prayers been answered in this grim way? And did she know now what he had really thought? Dark thought. Where was she now? What was she thinking now if she knew? Would she hate him — haunt him? It was not dawn yet, only two or three in the morning, and the moon was still bright. And in the next room she was lying, pale and cool, gone forever now out of his life.

He got up after a time and went forward into that pleasant front room where he had so often loved to sit, then back into her room to view the body again. Now that she was gone, here more than else-where, in her dead presence, he seemed better able to collect his scattered thoughts. She might see or she might not — might know or not. It was all over now. Only he could not help but feel a little evil. She had been so faithful, if nothing more, so earnest in behalf of him and of his children. He might have spared her these last dark thoughts of these last few days. His feelings were so jumbled that he could not place them half the time. But at the same time the ethics of the past, of his own irritated feelings and moods in regard to her, had to be adjusted somehow before he could have peace. They must be ad-justed, only how — how? He and Mrs. Elfridge had agreed not to disturb Doctor Storm any more to-night. They were all agreed to get what rest they could against the morning.

After a time he came forward once more to the front room to sit and gaze at the park. Here, perhaps, he could solve these mysteries for himself, think them out, find out what he did feel. He was evil for having wished all he had, that he knew and felt. And yet there was his own story, too — his life. The dawn was breaking by now; a faint grayness shaded the east and dimly lightened this room. A tall pier mirror between two windows now revealed him to himself — spare, angular, disheveled, his beard and hair astray and his eyes weary. The figure he made here as against his dreams of a happier life, once he were free, now struck him forcibly. What a farce! What a failure! Why should he, of all people, think of further happiness in love, even if he were free? Look at his reflection here in this mirror. What a picture — old, grizzled, done for! Had he not known that for so long? Was it not too ridiculous? Why should he have tolerated such vain thoughts? What could he of all people hope for now? No thing of beauty would have him now. Of course not. That glorious dream of his youth was gone forever. It was a mirage, an ignis fatuus. His wife might just as well have lived as died, for all the difference it would or could make to him. Only, he was really free just the same, almost as it were in spite of his varying moods. But he was old, weary, done for, a recluse and ungainly.

Now the innate cruelty of life, its blazing ironic indifference to him and so many grew rapidly upon him. What had he had? What all had he not missed? Dismally he stared first at his dark wrinkled skin; the crow's-feet at the sides of his eyes; the wrinkles across his forehead and between the eyes; his long, dark, wrinkled hands — handsome hands they once were, he thought; his angular, stiff body. Once he had been very much of a personage, he thought, striking, forceful, dynamic — but now! He turned and looked out over the park where the young trees were, and the lake, to the pinking dawn — just a trace now — a significant thing in itself at this hour surely — the new dawn, so wondrously new for younger people — then back at himself. What could he wish for now — what hope for?

As he did so his dream came back to him — that strange dream of seeking and being led and promised and yet always being led forward into a dimmer, darker land. What did that mean? Had it any real significance? Was it all to be dimmer, darker still? Was it typical of his life? He pondered.

"Free!" he said after a time. "Free! I know now how that is. I am free now, at last! Free! . . . Free! . . . Yes — free . . . to die!"

So he stood there ruminating and smoothing his hair and his beard.

Nigger Jeff[1]

THE CITY EDITOR was waiting for one of his best reporters, Elmer Davies by name, a vain and rather self-sufficient youth who was inclined to be of that turn of mind which sees in life only a fixed and ordered process of rewards and punishments. If one did not do exactly right, one did not get along well. On the contrary, if one did, one did. Only the so-called evil were really punished, only the good truly rewarded — or Mr. Davies had heard this so long in his youth that he had come nearly to believe it. Presently he appeared. He was dressed in a new spring suit, a new hat and new shoes. In the lapel of his coat was a small bunch of violets. It was one o'clock of a sunny spring afternoon, and he was feeling exceedingly well and good-natured — quite fit, indeed. The world was going unusually well with him. It seemed worth singing about.

"Read that, Davies," said the city editor, handing him the clipping. "I'll tell you afterward what I want you to do."

The reporter stood by the editorial chair and read:

Pleasant Valley, Ko., April 16.
"A most dastardly crime has just been reported here. Jeff Ingalls, a negro, this morning assaulted Ada Whitaker, the nineteen-year-old daughter of Morgan Whitaker, a well-to-do farmer, whose home is four miles south of this place. A posse, headed by Sheriff Mathews, has started in pursuit. If he is caught, it is thought he will be lynched."

The reporter raised his eyes as he finished. What a terrible crime! What evil people there were in the world! No doubt such a creature ought to be lynched, and that quickly.

"You had better go out there, Davies," said the city editor. "It looks as if something might come of that. A lynching up here would be a big thing. There's never been one in this state."

Davies smiled. He was always pleased to be sent out of town. It was a

---

1. "Nigger Jeff" first appeared in *Ainslee's*, November 1901.

mark of appreciation. The city editor rarely sent any of the other men on these big stories. What a nice ride he would have!

As he went along, however, a few minutes later he began to meditate on this. Perhaps, as the city editor had suggested, he might be compelled to witness an actual lynching. That was by no means so pleasant in itself. In his fixed code of rewards and punishments he had no particular place for lynchings, even for crimes of the nature described, especially if he had to witness the lynching. It was too horrible a kind of reward or punishment. Once, in line of duty, he had been compelled to witness a hanging, and that had made him sick — deathly so — even though carried out as a part of the due process of law of his day and place. Now, as he looked at this fine day and his excellent clothes, he was not so sure that this was a worthwhile assignment. Why should he always be selected for such things — just because he could write? There were others — lots of men on the staff. He began to hope as he went along that nothing really serious would come of it, that they would catch the man before he got there and put him in jail — or, if the worst had to be — painful thought! — that it would be all over by the time he got there. Let's see — the telegram had been filed at nine a.m. It was now one-thirty and would be three by the time he got out there, all of that. That would give them time enough, and then, if all were well, or ill, as it were, he could just gather the details of the crime and the — aftermath — and return. The mere thought of an approaching lynching troubled him greatly, and the farther he went the less he liked it.

He found the village of Pleasant Valley a very small affair indeed, just a few dozen houses nestling between green slopes of low hills, with one small business corner and a rambling array of lanes. One or two merchants of K——, the city from which he had just arrived, lived out here, but otherwise it was very rural. He took notes of the whiteness of the little houses, the shimmering beauty of the small stream one had to cross in going from the depot. At the one main corner a few men were gathered about a typical village barroom. Davies headed for this as being the most likely source of information.

In mingling with this company at first he said nothing about his being a newspaper man, being very doubtful as to its effect upon them, their freedom of speech and manner.

The whole company was apparently tense with interest in the crime which still remained unpunished, seemingly craving excitement and desirous of seeing something done about it. No such opportunity to work up wrath and vent their stored-up animal propensities had probably occurred here in years. He took this occasion to inquire into the exact details of the attack, where it had occurred, where the Whitakers lived. Then, seeing that mere talk prevailed here, he went away thinking that he had best find out for himself how the victim was. As yet she had not been described, and it was necessary to know a little something about her. Accordingly, he sought an old man who kept a stable in the village, and procured a horse. No carriage was to be had. Davies was not an excellent rider, but he made a shift of it. The Whitaker home was not so very far away — about four miles out — and before long he was knocking at its front door, set back a hundred feet from the rough country road.

"I'm from the *Times*," he said to the tall, raw-boned woman who opened the door, with an attempt at being impressive. His position as reporter in this matter was a little dubious; he might be welcome, and he might not. Then he asked if this were Mrs. Whitaker, and how Miss Whitaker was by now.

"She's doing very well," answered the woman, who seemed decidedly stern, if repressed and nervous, a Spartan type. "Won't you come in? She's rather feverish, but the doctor says she'll probably be all right later on." She said no more.

Davies acknowledged the invitation by entering. He was very anxious to see the girl, but she was sleeping under the influence of an opiate, and he did not care to press the matter at once.

"When did this happen?" he asked.

"About eight o'clock this morning," said the woman. "She started to go over to our next door neighbor here, Mr. Edmonds, and this negro met her. We didn't know anything about it until she came crying through the gate and dropped down in here."

"Were you the first one to meet her?" asked Davies.

"Yes, I was the only one," said Mrs. Whitaker. "The men had all gone to the fields."

Davies listened to more of the details, the type and history of the man, and then rose to go. Before doing so he was allowed to have a look at the girl, who was still sleeping. She was young and rather pretty. In the yard he met a country man who was just coming to get home news. The latter imparted more information.

"They're lookin' all around south of here," he said, speaking of a crowd which was supposed to be searching. "I expect they'll make short work of him if they get him. He can't get away very well, for he's on foot, wherever he is. The sheriff's after him too, with a deputy or two, I believe. He'll be tryin' to save him an' take him over to Clayton, but I don't believe he'll be able to do it, not if the crowd catches him first."

So, thought Davies, he would probably have to witness a lynching after all. The prospect was most unhappy.

"Does any one know where this negro lived?" he asked heavily, a growing sense of his duty weighing upon him.

"Oh, right down here a little way," replied the farmer. "Jeff Ingalls was his name. We all know him around here. He worked for one and another of the farmers hereabouts, and don't appear to have had such a bad record, either, except for drinkin' a little now and then. Miss Ada recognized him, all right. You follow this road to the next crossing and turn to the right. It's a little log house that sets back off the road — something like that one you see down the lane there, only it's got lots o' chips scattered about."

Davies decided to go there first, but changed his mind. It was growing late, and he thought he had better return to the village. Perhaps by now developments in connection with the sheriff or the posse were to be learned.

Accordingly, he rode back and put the horse in the hands of its owner, hoping that all had been concluded and that he might learn of it here. At the principal corner much the same company was still present, arguing, fomenting, gesticulating. They seemed parts of different companies that earlier in the day had been out searching. He wondered what they had been doing since, and then decided to ingratiate himself by telling them he had just come from the Whitakers and what he had learned there of the present condition of the girl and the movements of the sheriff.

Just then a young farmer came galloping up. He was coatless, hatless, breathless.

"They've got him!" he shouted excitedly. "They've got him!"

A chorus of "whos," "wheres" and "whens" greeted this information as the crowd gathered about the rider.

"Why, Mathews caught him up here at his own house!" exclaimed the latter, pulling out a handkerchief and wiping his face. "He must 'a' gone back there for something. Mathews's takin' him over to Clayton, so they think, but they don't project he'll ever get there. They're after him now, but Mathews says he'll shoot the first man that tries to take him away."

"Which way'd he go?" exclaimed the men in chorus, stirring as if to make an attack.

" 'Cross Sellers' Lane," said the rider. "The boys think he's goin' by way of Baldwin."

"Whoopee!" yelled one of the listeners. "We'll get him away from him, all right! Are you goin', Sam?"

"You bet!" said the latter. "Wait'll I get my horse!"

"Lord!" thought Davies. "To think of being (perforce) one of a lynching party — a hired spectator!"

He delayed no longer, however, but hastened to secure his horse again. He saw that the crowd would be off in a minute to catch up with the sheriff. There would be information in that quarter, drama very likely.

"What's doin'?" inquired the liveryman as he noted Davies' excited appearance.

"They're after him," replied the latter nervously. "The sheriff's caught him. They're going now to try to take him away from him, or that's what they say. The sheriff is taking him over to Clayton, by way of Baldwin. I want to get over there if I can. Give me the horse again, and I'll give you a couple of dollars more."

The liveryman led the horse out, but not without many provisionary cautions as to the care which was to be taken of him, the damages which would ensue if it were not. He was not to be ridden beyond midnight. If one were wanted for longer than that Davies must get him elsewhere or come and get another, to all of which Davies promptly agreed. He then mounted and rode away.

When he reached the corner again several of the men who had gone for their horses were already there, ready to start. The young man who had brought the news had long since dashed off to other parts.

Davies waited to see which road this new company would take. Then through as pleasant a country as one would wish to see, up hill and down dale, with charming vistas breaking upon the gaze at every turn, he did the riding of his life. So disturbed was the reporter by the grim turn things had taken that he scarcely noted the beauty that was stretched before him, save to note that it was so. Death! Death! The proximity of involuntary and enforced death was what weighed upon him now.

In about an hour the company had come in sight of the sheriff, who, with two other men, was driving a wagon he had borrowed along a lone country road. The latter was sitting at the back, a revolver in each hand, his face toward the group, which at sight of him trailed after at a respectful distance. Excited as every one was, there was no disposition, for the time being at least, to halt the progress of the law.

"He's in that wagon," Davies heard one man say. "Don't you see they've got him in there tied and laid down?"

Davies looked.

"That's right," said another. "I see him now."

"What we ought to do," said a third, who was riding near the front, "is to take him away and hang him. That's just what he deserves, and that's what he'll get before we're through to-day."

"Yes!" called the sheriff, who seemed to have heard this. "You're not goin' to do any hangin' this day, so you just might as well go on back." He did not appear to be much troubled by the appearance of the crowd.

"Where's old man Whitaker?" asked one of the men who seemed to feel that they needed a leader. "He'd get him quick enough!"

"He's with the other crowd, down below Olney," was the reply.

"Somebody ought to go an' tell him."

"Clark's gone," assured another, who hoped for the worst.

Davies rode among the company a prey to mingled and singular feelings. He was very much excited and yet depressed by the character of the crowd which, in so far as he could see, was largely impelled to its jaunt by curiosity and yet also able under sufficient motivation on the part of some one — any one, really — to kill too. There was not so much daring as a desire to gain daring from others, an unconscious wish or impulse to organize the total strength or will of those present into one strength or one will, sufficient to overcome the sheriff and inflict death upon his charge. It was strange — almost intellectually incomprehensible — and yet so it was. The men were plainly afraid of the determined sheriff. They thought something ought to be done, but they did not feel like getting into trouble.

Mathews, a large solemn, sage, brown man in worn clothes and a faded brown hat, contemplated the recent addition to his trailers with apparent indifference. Seemingly he was determined to protect his man and avoid mob justice, come what may. A mob should not have him if he had to shoot, and if he shot it would be to kill. Finally, since the company thus added to did not dash upon him, he seemingly decided to scare them off. Apparently he thought he could do this, since they trailed like calves.

"Stop a minute!" he called to his driver.

The latter pulled up. So did the crowd behind. Then the sheriff stood over the prostrate body of the negro, who lay in the jolting wagon beneath him, and called back:

"Go 'way from here, you people! Go on, now! I won't have you follerin' after me!"

"Give us the nigger!" yelled one in a half-bantering, half-derisive tone of voice.

"I'll give ye just two minutes to go on back out o' this road," returned the sheriff grimly, pulling out his watch and looking at it. They were about a hundred feet apart. "If you don't, I'll clear you out!"

"Give us the nigger!"

"I know you, Scott," answered Mathews, recognizing the voice. "I'll arrest every last one of ye to-morrow. Mark my word!"

The company listened in silence, the horses champing and twisting.

"We've got a right to foller," answered one of the men.

"I give ye fair warning," said the sheriff, jumping from his wagon and leveling his pistols as he approached. "When I count five I'll begin to shoot!"

He was a serious and stalwart figure as he approached, and the crowd fell back a little.

"Git out o' this now!" he yelled. "One — Two — "

The company turned completely and retreated, Davies among them.

"We'll foller him when he gits further on," said one of the men in explanation.

"He's got to do it," said another. "Let him git a little ways ahead."

The sheriff returned to his wagon and drove on. He seemed, however, to realize that he would not be obeyed and that safety lay in haste alone. His wagon was traveling fast. If only he could lose them or get a good start he might possibly get to Clayton and the strong county jail by morning. His followers, however, trailed him swiftly as might be, determined not to be left behind.

"He's goin' to Baldwin," said one of the company of which Davies was a member.

"Where's that?" asked Davies.

"Over west o' here, about four miles."

"Why is he going there?"

"That's where he lives. I guess he thinks if he kin git 'im over there he kin purtect 'im till he kin git more help from Clayton. I cal'late he'll try an' take 'im over yet to-night, or early in the mornin' shore."

Davies smiled at the man's English. This countryside lingo always fascinated him.

Yet the men lagged, hesitating as to what to do. They did not want to lose sight of Mathews, and yet cowardice controlled them. They did not want to get into direct altercation with the law. It wasn't their place to hang the man, although plainly they felt that he ought to be hanged, and that it would be a stirring and exciting thing if he were. Consequently they desired to watch and be on hand — to get old Whitaker and his son Jake, if they could, who were out looking elsewhere. They wanted to see what the father and brother would do.

The quandary was solved by one of the men, who suggested that they could get to Baldwin by going back to Pleasant Valley and taking the Sand River pike, and that in the meantime they might come upon Whitaker and his son en route, or leave word at his house. It was a shorter cut than this the sheriff was taking, although he would get there first now. Possibly they could beat him at least to Clayton, if he attempted to go on. The Clayton road was back via Pleasant Valley, or

near it, and easily intercepted. Therefore, while one or two remained to
trail the sheriff and give the alarm in case he did attempt to go on to
Clayton, the rest, followed by Davies, set off at a gallop to Pleasant Valley.
It was nearly dusk now when they arrived and stopped at the corner
store — supper time. The fires of evening meals were marked by upcurl-
ing smoke from chimneys. Here, somehow, the zest to follow seemed to
depart. Evidently the sheriff had worsted them for the night. Morg
Whitaker, the father, had not been found; neither had Jake. Perhaps they
had better eat. Two or three had already secretly fallen away.

They were telling the news of what had occurred so far to one of the
two storekeepers who kept the place, when suddenly Jake Whitaker, the
girl's brother, and several companions came riding up. They had been
scouring the territory to the north of the town, and were hot and tired.
Plainly they were unaware of the developments of which the crowd had
been a part.

"The sheriff's got 'im!" exclaimed one of the company, with that
blatance which always accompanies the telling of great news in small
rural companies. "He taken him over to Baldwin in a wagon a coupla
hours ago."

"Which way did he go?" asked the son, whose hardy figure, worn,
hand-me-down clothes and rakish hat showed up picturesquely as he
turned here and there on his horse.

" 'Cross Seller' Lane. You won't git 'em that-a-way, though, Jake. He's
already over there by now. Better take the short cut."

A babble of voices now made the scene more interesting. One told
how the negro had been caught, another that the sheriff was defiant, a
third that men were still tracking him or over there watching, until all
the chief points of the drama had been spoken if not heard.

Instantly suppers were forgotten. The whole customary order of the
evening was overturned once more. The company started off on another
excited jaunt, up hill and down dale, through the lovely country that lay
between Baldwin and Pleasant Valley.

By now Davies was very weary of this procedure and of his saddle. He
wondered when, if ever, this story was to culminate, let alone he write it.
Tragic as it might prove, he could not nevertheless spend an indefinite
period trailing a possibility, and yet, so great was the potentiality of the
present situation, he dared not leave. By contrast with the horror impending, as he now noted, the night was so beautiful that it was all but
poignant. Stars were already beginning to shine. Distant lamps twinkled
like yellow eyes from the cottages in the valleys and on the hillsides. The
air was fresh and tender. Some pea-fowls were crying afar off, and the
east promised a golden moon.

Silently the assembled company trotted on — no more than a score in all. In the dusk, and with Jake ahead, it seemed too grim a pilgrimage for joking. Young Jake, riding silently toward the front, looked as if tragedy were all he craved. His friends seemed considerately to withdraw from him, seeing that he was the aggrieved.

After an hour's riding Baldwin came into view, lying in a sheltering cup of low hills. Already its lights were twinkling softly and there was still an air of honest firesides and cheery suppers about it which appealed to Davies in his hungry state. Still, he had no thought now of anything save this pursuit.

Once in the village, the company was greeted by calls of recognition. Everybody seemed to know what they had come for. The sheriff and his charge were still there, so a dozen citizens volunteered. The local storekeepers and loungers followed the cavalcade up the street to the sheriff's house, for the riders had now fallen into a solemn walk.

"You won't get him though, boys," said one whom Davies later learned was Seavey, the village postmaster and telegraph operator, a rather youthful person of between twenty-five and thirty, as they passed his door. "He's got two deputies in there with him, or did have, and they say he's going to take him over to Clayton."

At the first street corner they were joined by the several men who had followed the sheriff.

"He tried to give us the slip," they volunteered excitedly, "but he's got the nigger in the house, there, down in the cellar. The deputies ain't with him. They've gone somewhere for help — Clayton, maybe."

"How do you know?"

"We saw 'em go out that back way. We think we did, anyhow."

A hundred feet from the sheriff's little white cottage, which backed up against a sloping field, the men parleyed. Then Jake announced that he proposed to go boldly up to the sheriff's door and demand the negro.

"If he don't turn him out I'll break in the door an' take him!" he said.

"That's right! We'll stand by you, Whitaker," commented several.

By now the throng of unmounted natives had gathered. The whole village was up and about, its one street alive and running with people. Heads appeared at doors and windows. Riders pranced up and down, hallooing. A few revolver shots were heard. Presently the mob gathered even closer to the sheriff's gate, and Jake stepped forward as leader. Instead, however, of going boldly up to the door as at first it appeared he would, he stopped at the gate, calling to the sheriff.

"Hello, Mathews!"

"Eh, eh, eh!" bellowed the crowd.

The call was repeated. Still no answer. Apparently to the sheriff delay appeared to be his one best weapon.

Their coming, however, was not as unexpected as some might have thought. The figure of the sheriff was plainly to be seen close to one of the front windows. He appeared to be holding a double-barreled shotgun. The negro, as it developed later, was cowering and chattering in the darkest corner of the cellar, hearkening no doubt to the voices and firing of the revolvers outside.

Suddenly, and just as Jake was about to go forward, the front door of the house flew open, and in the glow of a single lamp inside appeared first the double-barreled end of the gun, followed immediately by the form of Mathews, who held the weapon poised ready for a quick throw to the shoulder. All except Jake fell back.

"Mr. Mathews," he called deliberately, "we want that nigger!"

"Well, you can't git 'im!" replied the sheriff. "He's not here."

"Then what you got that gun fer?" yelled a voice.

Mathews made no answer.

"Better give him up, Mathews," called another, who was safe in the crowd, "or we'll come in an' take him!"

"No you won't," said the sheriff defiantly. "I said the man wasn't here. I say it ag'in. You couldn't have him if he was, an' you can't come in my house! Now if you people don't want trouble you'd better go on away."

"He's down in the cellar!" yelled another.

"Why don't you let us see?" asked another.

Mathews waved his gun slightly.

"You'd better go away from here now," cautioned the sheriff. "I'm tellin' ye! I'll have warrants out for the lot o' ye, if ye don't mind!"

The crowd continued to simmer and stew, while Jake stood as before. He was very pale and tense, but lacked initiative.

"He won't shoot," called some one at the back of the crowd. "Why don't you go in, Jake, an' git him?"

"Sure! Rush in. That's it!" observed a second.

"He won't, eh?" replied the sheriff softly. Then he added in a lower tone, "The first man that comes inside that gate takes the consequences."

No one ventured inside the gate; many even fell back. It seemed as if the planned assault had come to nothing.

"Why not go around the back way?" called some one else.

"Try it!" replied the sheriff. "See what you find on that side! I told you you couldn't come inside. You'd better go away from here now before ye git into trouble," he repeated. "You can't come in, an' it'll only mean bloodshed."

There was more chattering and jesting while the sheriff stood on guard. He, however, said no more. Nor did he allow the banter, turmoil and lust for tragedy to disturb him. Only, he kept his eye on Jake, on whose movements the crowd seemed to hang.

Time passed, and still nothing was done. The truth was that young Jake, put to the test, was not sufficiently courageous himself, for all his daring, and felt the weakness of the crowd behind him. To all intents and purposes he was alone, for he did not inspire confidence. He finally fell back a little, observing, "I'll git 'im before mornin', all right," and now the crowd itself began to disperse, returning to its stores and homes or standing about the postoffice and the one village drugstore. Finally, Davies smiled and came away. He was sure he had the story of a defeated mob. The sheriff was to be his great hero. He proposed to interview him later. For the present, he meant to seek out Seavey, the telegraph operator, and arrange to file a message, then see if something to eat was not to be had somewhere.

After a time he found the operator and told him what he wanted — to write and file a story as he wrote it. The latter indicated a table in the little postoffice and telegraph station which he could use. He became very much interested in the reporter when he learned he was from the *Times*, and when Davies asked where he could get something to eat said he would run across the street and tell the proprietor of the only boarding house to fix him something which he could consume as he wrote. He appeared to be interested in how a newspaper man would go about telling a story of this kind over a wire.

"You start your story," he said, "and I'll come back and see if I can get the *Times* on the wire."

Davies sat down and began his account. He was intent on describing things to date, the uncertainty and turmoil, the apparent victory of the sheriff. Plainly the courage of the latter had won, and it was all so picturesque. "A foiled lynching," he began, and as he wrote the obliging postmaster, who had by now returned, picked up the pages and carefully deciphered them for himself.

"That's all right. I'll see if I can get the *Times* now," he commented.

"Very obliging postmaster," thought Davies as he wrote, but he had so often encountered pleasant and obliging people on his rounds that he soon dropped that thought.

The food was brought, and still Davies wrote on, munching as he did so. In a little while the *Times* answered an often-repeated call.

"Davies at Baldwin," ticked the postmaster, "get ready for quite a story!"

"Let 'er go!" answered the operator at the *Times*, who had been expecting this dispatch.

As the events of the day formulated themselves in his mind, Davies wrote and turned over page after page. Between whiles he looked out through the small window before him where afar off he could see a lonely light twinkling against a hillside. Not infrequently he stopped his work to see if anything new was happening, whether the situation was in any danger of changing, but apparently it was not. He then proposed to remain until all possibility of a tragedy, this night anyhow, was eliminated. The operator also wandered about, waiting for an accumulation of pages upon which he could work but making sure to keep up with the writer. The two became quite friendly.

Finally, his dispatch nearly finished, he asked the postmaster to caution the night editor at K—— to the effect, that if anything more happened before one in the morning he would file it, but not to expect anything more as nothing might happen. The reply came that he was to remain and await developments. Then he and the postmaster sat down to talk.

About eleven o'clock, when both had about convinced themselves that all was over for this night anyhow, and the lights in the village had all but vanished, a stillness of the purest, summery-est, country-est quality having settled down, a faint beating of hoofs, which seemed to suggest the approach of a large cavalcade, could be heard out on the Sand River pike as Davies by now had come to learn it was, back or northwest of the postoffice. At the sound the postmaster got up, as did Davies, both stepping outside and listening. On it came, and as the volume increased, the former said, "Might be help for the sheriff, but I doubt it. I telegraphed Clayton six times to-day. They wouldn't come that way, though. It's the wrong road." Now, thought Davies nervously, after all there might be something to add to his story, and he had so wished that it was all over! Lynchings, as he now felt, were horrible things. He wished people wouldn't do such things — take the law, which now more than ever he respected, into their own hands. It was too brutal, cruel. That negro cowering there in the dark probably, and the sheriff all taut and tense, worrying over his charge and his duty, were not happy things to contemplate in the face of such a thing as this. It was true that the crime which had been committed was dreadful, but still why couldn't people allow the law to take its course? It was so much better. The law was powerful enough to deal with cases of this kind.

"They're comin' back, all right," said the postmaster solemnly, as he and Davies stared in the direction of the sound which grew louder from moment to moment.

"It's not any help from Clayton, I'm afraid."

"By George, I think you're right!" answered the reporter, something telling him that more trouble was at hand. "Here they come!"

As he spoke there was a clattering of hoofs and crunching of saddle girths as a large company of men dashed up the road and turned into the narrow street of the village, the figure of Jake Whitaker and an older bearded man in a wide black hat riding side by side in front.

"There's Jake," said the postmaster, "and that's his father riding beside him there. The old man's a terror when he gets his dander up. Sompin's sure to happen now."

Davies realized that in his absence writing a new turn had been given to things. Evidently the son had returned to Pleasant Valley and organized a new posse or gone out to meet his father.

Instantly the place was astir again. Lights appeared in doorways and windows, and both were thrown open. People were leaning or gazing out to see what new movement was afoot. Davies noted at once that there was none of the brash enthusiasm about this company such as had characterized the previous descent. There was grimness everywhere, and he now began to feel that this was the beginning of the end. After the cavalcade had passed down the street toward the sheriff's house, which was quite dark now, he ran after it, arriving a few moments after the former which was already in part dismounted. The townspeople followed. The sheriff, as it now developed, had not relaxed any of his vigilance, however; he was not sleeping, and as the crowd reappeared the light inside reappeared.

By the light of the moon, which was almost overhead, Davies was able to make out several of his companions of the afternoon, and Jake, the son. There were many more, though, now, whom he did not know, and foremost among them this old man.

The latter was strong, iron-gray, and wore a full beard. He looked very much like a blacksmith.

"Keep your eye on the old man," advised the postmaster, who had by now come up and was standing by.

While they were still looking, the old man went boldly forward to the little front porch of the house and knocked at the door. Some one lifted a curtain at the window and peeped out.

"Hello, in there!" cried the old man, knocking again.

"What do you want?" asked a voice.

"I want that nigger!"

"Well, you can't have him! I've told you people that once."

"Bring him out or I'll break down the door!" said the old man.

"If you do it's at your own risk. I know you, Whitaker, an' you know me. I'll give ye two minutes to get off that porch!"

"I want that nigger, I tell ye!"

"If ye don't git off that porch I'll fire through the door," said the voice solemnly. "One — Two ——"

The old man backed cautiously away.

"Come out, Mathews!" yelled the crowd. "You've got to give him up this time. We ain't goin' back without him."

Slowly the door opened, as if the individual within were very well satisfied as to his power to handle the mob. He had done it once before this night, why not again? It revealed his tall form, armed with his shotgun. He looked around very stolidly, and then addressed the old man as one would a friend.

"Ye can't have him, Morgan," he said. "It's ag'in' the law. You know that as well as I do."

"Law or no law," said the old man, "I want that nigger!"

"I tell you I can't let you have him, Morgan. It's ag'in' the law. You know you oughtn't to be comin' around here at this time o' night actin' so."

"Well, I'll take him then," said the old man, making a move.

"Stand back!" shouted the sheriff, leveling his gun on the instant. "I'll blow ye into kingdom come, sure as hell!"

A noticeable movement on the part of the crowd ceased. The sheriff lowered his weapon as if he thought the danger were once more over.

"You-all ought to be ashamed of yerselves," he went on, his voice sinking to a gentle neighborly reproof, "tryin' to upset the law this way."

"The nigger didn't upset no law, did he?" asked one derisively.

"Well, the law's goin' to take care of the nigger now," Mathews made answer.

"Give us that scoundrel, Mathews; you'd better do it," said the old man. "It'll save a heap o' trouble."

"I'll not argue with ye, Morgan. I said ye couldn't have him, an' ye can't. If ye want bloodshed, all right. But don't blame me. I'll kill the first man that tries to make a move this way."

He shifted his gun handily and waited. The crowd stood outside his little fence murmuring.

Presently the old man retired and spoke to several others. There was more murmuring, and then he came back to the dead line.

"We don't want to cause trouble, Mathews," he began explanatively, moving his hand oratorically, "but we think you ought to see that it won't do any good to stand out. We think that ——"

Davies and the postmaster were watching young Jake, whose peculiar attitude attracted their attention. The latter was standing poised at the edge of the crowd, evidently seeking to remain unobserved. His eyes were on the sheriff, who was hearkening to the old man. Suddenly, as the father talked and when the sheriff seemed for a moment mollified and unsuspecting, he made a quick run for the porch. There was an intense movement all along the line as the life and death of the deed became apparent. Quickly the sheriff drew his gun to his shoulder. Both triggers were pressed at the same time, and the gun spoke, but not before Jake was in and under him. The latter had been in sufficient time to knock the gun barrel upward and fall upon his man. Both shots blazed harmlessly over the heads of the crowd in red puffs, and then followed a general onslaught. Men leaped the fence by tens and crowded upon the little cottage. They swarmed about every side of the house and crowded upon the porch, where four men were scuffling with the sheriff. The latter soon gave up, vowing vengeance and the law. Torches were brought, and a rope. A wagon drove up and was backed into the yard. Then began the calls for the negro.

As Davies contemplated all this he could not help thinking of the negro who during all this turmoil must have been crouching in his corner in the cellar, trembling for his fate. Now indeed he must realize that his end was near. He could not have dozed or lost consciousness during the intervening hours, but must have been cowering there, wondering and praying. All the while he must have been terrified lest the sheriff might not get him away in time. Now, at the sound of horses' feet and the new murmurs of contention, how must his body quake and his teeth chatter!

"I'd hate to be that nigger," commented the postmaster grimly, "but you can't do anything with 'em. The county oughta sent help."

"It's horrible, horrible!" was all Davies could say.

He moved closer to the house, with the crowd, eager to observe every detail of the procedure. Now it was that a number of the men, as eager in their search as bloodhounds, appeared at a low cellar entryway at the side of the house carrying a rope. Others followed with torches. Headed by father and son they began to descend into the dark hole. With impressive daring, Davies, who was by no means sure that he would be allowed but who was also determined if possible to see, followed.

Suddenly, in the farthest corner, he espied Ingalls. The latter in his fear and agony had worked himself into a crouching position, as if he were about to spring. His nails were apparently forced into the earth. His eyes were rolling, his mouth foaming.

"Oh, my Lawd, boss," he moaned, gazing almost as one blind, at the lights, "oh, my Lawd, boss, don't kill me! I won't do it no mo'. I didn't go to do it. I didn't mean to dis time. I was just drunk, boss. Oh, my Lawd! My Lawd!" His teeth chattered the while his mouth seemed to gape open. He was no longer sane really, but kept repeating monotonously, "Oh, my Lawd!"

"Here he is, boys! Pull him out," cried the father.

The negro now gave one yell of terror and collapsed, falling prone. He quite bounded as he did so, coming down with a dead chug on the earthen floor. Reason had forsaken him. He was by now a groveling, foaming brute. The last gleam of intelligence was that which notified him of the set eyes of his pursuers.

Davies, who by now had retreated to the grass outside before this sight, was standing but ten feet back when they began to reappear after seizing and binding him. Although shaken to the roots of his being, he still had all the cool observing powers of the trained and relentless reporter. Even now he noted the color values of the scene, the red, smoky heads of the torches, the disheveled appearance of the men, the scuffling and pulling. Then all at once he clapped his hands over his mouth, almost unconscious of what he was doing.

"Oh, my God!" he whispered, his voice losing power.

The sickening sight was that of the negro, foaming at the mouth, bloodshot as to his eyes, his hands working convulsively, being dragged up the cellar steps feet foremost. They had tied a rope about his waist and feet, and so had hauled him out, leaving his head to hang and drag. The black face was distorted beyond all human semblance.

"Oh, my God!" said Davies again, biting his fingers unconsciously.

The crowd gathered about now more closely than ever, more horror-stricken than gleeful at their own work. None apparently had either the courage or the charity to gainsay what was being done. With a kind of mechanical deftness now the negro was rudely lifted and like a sack of wheat thrown into the wagon. Father and son now mounted in front to drive and the crowd took to their horses, content to clatter, a silent cavalcade, behind. As Davies afterwards concluded, they were not so much hardened lynchers perhaps as curious spectators, the majority of them, eager for any variation — any excuse for one — to the dreary commonplaces of their existences. The task to most — all indeed — was entirely new. Wide-eyed and nerve-racked, Davies ran for his own horse and mounting followed. He was so excited he scarcely knew what he was doing.

Slowly the silent company now took its way up the Sand River pike whence it had come. The moon was still high, pouring down a wash of silvery light. As Davies rode he wondered how he was to complete his telegram, but decided that he could not. When this was over there would be no time. How long would it be before they would really hang him? And would they? The whole procedure seemed so unreal, so barbaric that he could scarcely believe it — that he was a part of it. Still they rode on.

"Are they really going to hang him?" he asked of one who rode beside him, a total stranger who seemed however not to resent his presence.

"That's what they got 'im fer," answered the stranger.

And think, he thought to himself, to-morrow night he would be resting in his own good bed back in K——!

Davies dropped behind again and into silence and tried to recover his nerves. He could scarcely realize that he, ordinarily accustomed to the routine of the city, its humdrum and at least outward social regularity, was a part of this. The night was so soft, the air so refreshing. The shadowy trees were stirring with a cool night wind. Why should any one have to die this way? Why couldn't the people of Baldwin or elsewhere have bestirred themselves on the side of the law before this, just let it take its course? Both father and son now seemed brutal, the injury to the daughter and sister not so vital as all this. Still, also, custom seemed to require death in this way for this. It was like some axiomatic, mathematic law — hard, but custom. The silent company, an articulated, mechanical and therefore terrible thing, moved on. It also was axiomatic, mathematic. After a time he drew near to the wagon and looked at the negro again.

The latter, as Davies was glad to note, seemed still out of his sense. He was breathing heavily and groaning, but probably not with any conscious pain. His eyes were fixed and staring, his face and hands bleeding as if they had been scratched or trampled upon. He was crumpled limply.

But Davies could stand it no longer now. He fell back, sick at heart, content to see no more. It seemed a ghastly, murderous thing to do. Still the company moved on and he followed, past fields lit white by the moon, under dark, silent groups of trees, through which the moonlight fell in patches, up low hills and down into valleys, until at last a little stream came into view, the same little stream, as it proved, which he had seen earlier to-day and for a bridge over which they were heading. Here it ran now, sparkling like electricity in the night. After a time the road drew closer to the water and then crossed directly over the bridge, which could be seen a little way ahead.

Up to this the company now rode and then halted. The wagon was driven up on the bridge, and father and son got out. All the riders, including Davies, dismounted, and a full score of them gathered about the wagon from which the negro was lifted, quite as one might a bag.

Fortunately, as Davies now told himself, he was still unconscious, an accidental mercy. Nevertheless he decided now that he could not witness the end, and went down by the waterside slightly above the bridge. He was not, after all, the utterly relentless reporter. From where he stood, however, he could see long beams of iron projecting out over the water, where the bridge was braced, and some of the men fastening a rope to a beam, and then he could see that they were fixing the other end around the negro's neck.

Finally the curious company stood back, and he turned his face away. "Have you anything to say?" a voice demanded.

There was no answer. The negro was probably lolling and groaning, quite as unconscious as he was before.

Then came the concerted action of a dozen men, the lifting of the black mass into the air, and then Davies saw the limp form plunge down and pull up with a creaking sound of rope. In the weak moonlight it seemed as if the body were struggling, but he could not tell. He watched, wide-mouthed and silent, and then the body ceased moving. Then after a time he heard the company making ready to depart, and finally it did so, leaving him quite indifferently to himself and his thoughts. Only the black mass swaying in the pale light over the glimmering water seemed human and alive, his sole companion.

He sat down upon the bank and gazed in silence. Now the horror was gone. The suffering was ended. He was no longer afraid. Everything was summery and beautiful. The whole cavalcade had disappeared; the moon finally sank. His horse, tethered to a sapling beyond the bridge, waited patiently. Still he sat. He might now have hurried back to the small postoffice in Baldwin and attempted to file additional details of this story, providing he could find Seavey, but it would have done no good. It was quite too late, and anyhow what did it matter? No other reporter had been present, and he could write a fuller, sadder, more colorful story on the morrow. He wondered idly what had become of Seavey? Why had he not followed? Life seemed so sad, so strange, so mysterious, so inexplicable.

As he still sat there the light of morning broke, a tender lavender and gray in the east. Then came the roseate hues of dawn, all the wondrous coloring of celestial halls, to which the waters of the stream responded. The white pebbles shone pinkily at the bottom, the grass and sedges first black now gleamed a translucent green. Still the body hung there black and limp against the sky, and now a light breeze sprang up and stirred it visibly. At last he arose, mounted his horse and made his way back to Pleasant Valley, too full of the late tragedy to be much interested in anything else. Rousing his liveryman, he adjusted his difficulties with him by telling him the whole story, assuring him of his horse's care and handing him a five-dollar bill. Then he left, to walk and think again.

Since there was no train before noon and his duty plainly called him to a portion of another day's work here, he decided to make a day of it, idling about and getting additional details as to what further might be done. Who would cut the body down? What about arresting the lynchers—the father and son, for instance? What about the sheriff now? Would he act as he threatened? If he telegraphed the main fact of the lynching his city editor would not mind, he knew, his coming late, and the day here was so beautiful. He proceeded to talk with citizens and officials, rode out to the injured girl's home, rode to Baldwin to see the sheriff. There was a singular silence and placidity in that corner. The latter assured him that he knew nearly all of those who had taken part, and proposed to swear out warrants for them, but just the same Davies noted that he took his defeat as he did his danger, philosophically. There was no real activity in that corner later. He wished to remain a popular sheriff, no doubt.

It was sundown again before he remembered that he had not discovered whether the body had been removed. Nor had he heard why the negro came back, nor exactly how he was caught. A nine o'clock evening train to the city giving him a little more time for investigation, he decided to avail himself of it. The negro's cabin was two miles out along a pine-shaded road, but so pleasant was the evening that he decided to walk. En route, the last rays of the sinking sun stretched long shadows of budding trees across his path. It was not long before he came upon the cabin, a one-story affair set well back from the road and surrounded with a few scattered trees. By now it was quite dark. The ground between the cabin and the road was open, and strewn with the chips of a wood-pile. The roof was sagged, and the windows patched in places, but for all that it had the glow of a home. Through the front door, which stood open, the blaze of a wood-fire might be seen, its yellow light filling the interior with a golden glow.

Hesitating before the door, Davies finally knocked. Receiving no answer he looked in on the battered cane chairs and aged furniture with considerable interest. It was a typical negro cabin, poor beyond the need of description. After a time a door in the rear of the room opened and a little negro girl entered carrying a battered tin lamp without any chimney. She had not heard his knock and started perceptibly at the sight of his figure in the doorway. Then she raised her smoking lamp above her head in order to see better, and approached.

There was something ridiculous about her unformed figure and loose gingham dress, as he noted. Her feet and hands were so large. Her black head was strongly emphasized by little pigtails of hair done up in white twine, which stood out all over her head. Her dark skin was made apparently more so by contrast with her white teeth and the whites of her eyes.

Davies looked at her for a moment but little moved now by the oddity which ordinarily would have amused him, and asked, "Is this where Ingalls lived?"

The girl nodded her head. She was exceedingly subdued, and looked as if she might have been crying.

"Has the body been brought here?"

"Yes, suh," she answered, with a soft negro accent.

"When did they bring it?"

"Dis moanin'."

"Are you his sister?"

"Yes, suh."

"Well, can you tell me how they caught him? When did he come back, and what for?" He was feeling slightly ashamed to intrude thus.

"In de afternoon, about two."

"And what for?" repeated Davies.

"To see us," answered the girl. "To see my motha'."

"Well, did he want anything? He didn't come just to see her, did he?"

"Yes, suh," said the girl, "he come to say good-by. We doan know when dey caught him." Her voice wavered.

"Well, didn't he know he might get caught?" asked Davies sympathetically, seeing that the girl was so moved.

"Yes, suh, I think he did."

She still stood very quietly holding the poor battered lamp up, and looking down.

"Well, what did he have to say?" asked Davies.

"He didn' have nothin' much to say, suh. He said he wanted to see motha'. He was a-goin' away."

The girl seemed to regard Davies as an official of some sort, and he knew it.

"Can I have a look at the body?" he asked.

The girl did not answer, but started as if to lead the way.

"When is the funeral?" he asked.

"Tomorra'."

The girl then led him through several bare sheds of rooms strung in a row to the furthermost one of the line. This last seemed a sort of storage shed for odds and ends. It had several windows, but they were quite bare of glass and open to the moonlight save for a few wooden boards nailed across from the outside. Davies had been wondering all the while where

the body was and at the lonely and forsaken air of the place. No one but
this little pig-tailed girl seemed about. If they had any colored neighbors
they were probably afraid to be seen here.

Now, as he stepped into this cool, dark, exposed outer room, the
desolation seemed quite complete. It was very bare, a mere shed or
wash-room. There was the body in the middle of the room, stretched
upon an ironing board which rested on a box and a chair, and covered
with a white sheet. All the corners of the room were quite dark. Only its
middle was brightened by splotches of silvery light.

Davies came forward, the while the girl left him, still carrying her
lamp. Evidently she thought the moon lighted up the room sufficiently,
and she did not feel equal to remaining. He lifted the sheet quite boldly,
for he could see well enough, and looked at the still, black form. The
face was extremely distorted, even in death, and he could see where the
rope had tightened. A bar of cool moonlight lay just across the face and
breast. He was still looking, thinking soon to restore the covering, when
a sound, half sigh, half groan, reached his ears.

At it he started as if a ghost had made it. It was so eerie and unexpected in this dark place. His muscles tightened. Instantly his heart went
hammering like mad. His first impression was that it must have come
from the dead.

"Oo-o-ohh!" came the sound again, this time whimpering, as if some
one were crying.

Instantly he turned, for now it seemed to come from a corner of the
room, the extreme corner to his right, back of him. Greatly disturbed, he
approached, and then as his eyes strained he seemed to catch the
shadow of something, the figure of a woman, perhaps, crouching against
the walls, huddled up, dark, almost indistinguishable.

"Oh, oh, oh!" the sound now repeated itself, even more plaintively
than before.

Davies began to understand. He approached slowly, then more swiftly
desired to withdraw, for he was in the presence of an old black mammy,
doubled up and weeping. She was in the very niche of the two walls, her
head sunk on her knees, her body quite still. "Oh, oh, oh!" she repeated,
as he stood there near her.

Davies drew silently back. Before such grief his intrusion seemed cold
and unwarranted. The guiltlessness of the mother — her love — how
could one balance that against the other? The sensation of tears came to
his eyes. He instantly covered the dead and withdrew.

Out in the moonlight he struck a brisk pace, but soon stopped and
looked back. The whole dreary cabin, with its one golden eye, the door,
seemed such a pitiful thing. The weeping mammy, alone in her

corner — and he had come back to say "Good-by!" Davies swelled with feeling. The night, the tragedy, the grief, he saw it all. But also with the cruel instinct of the budding artist that he already was, he was beginning to meditate on the character of story it would make — the color, the pathos. The knowledge now that it was not always exact justice that was meted out to all and that it was not so much the business of the writer to indict as to interpret was borne in on him with distinctness by the cruel sorrow of the mother, whose blame, if any, was infinitesimal.

"I'll get it all in!" he exclaimed feelingly, if triumphantly at last. "I'll get it all in!"

The Lost Phœbe[1]

THEY LIVED together in a part of the country which was not so prosperous as it had once been, about three miles from one of those small towns that, instead of increasing in population, is steadily decreasing. The territory was not very thickly settled; perhaps a house every other mile or so, with large areas of corn- and wheat-land and fallow fields that at odd seasons had been sown to timothy and clover. Their particular house was part log and part frame, the log portion being the old original home of Henry's grandfather. The new portion, of now rain-beaten, time-worn slabs, through which the wind squeaked in the chinks at times, and which several overshadowing elms and a butternut-tree made picturesque and reminiscently pathetic, but a little damp, was erected by Henry when he was twenty-one and just married.

That was forty-eight years before. The furniture inside, like the house outside, was old and mildewy and reminiscent of an earlier day. You have seen the what-not of cherry wood, perhaps, with spiral legs and fluted top. It was there. The old-fashioned four poster bed, with its ball-like protuberances and deep curving incisions, was there also, a sadly alienated descendant of an early Jacobean ancestor. The bureau of cherry was also high and wide and solidly built, but faded-looking, and with a musty odor. The rag carpet that underlay all these sturdy examples of enduring furniture was a weak, faded, lead-and-pink-colored affair woven by Phœbe Ann's own hands, when she was fifteen years younger than she was when she died. The creaky wooden loom on which it had been done now stood like a dusty, bony skeleton, along with a broken rocking-chair, a worm-eaten clothes-press — Heaven knows how old — a lime-stained bench that had once been used to keep flowers on outside the door, and other decrepit factors of household utility, in an east room that was a lean-to against this so-called main portion. All sorts of other broken-down furniture were about this place;

---

1. "The Lost Phœbe" first appeared in *The Century Magazine*, April 1916.

an antiquated clothes-horse, cracked in two of its ribs; a broken mirror in an old cherry frame, which had fallen from a nail and cracked itself three days before their youngest son, Jerry, died; an extension hat-rack, which once had had porcelain knobs on the ends of its pegs; and a sewing-machine, long since outdone in its clumsy mechanism by rivals of a newer generation.

The orchard to the east of the house was full of gnarled old apple-trees, worm-eaten as to trunks and branches, and fully ornamented with green and white lichens, so that it had a sad, greenish-white, silvery effect in moonlight. The low outhouses, which had once housed chickens, a horse or two, a cow, and several pigs, were covered with patches of moss as to their roof, and the sides had been free of paint for so long that they were blackish gray as to color, and a little spongy. The picket-fence in front, with its gate squeaky and askew, and the side fences of the stake-and-rider type were in an equally run-down condition. As a matter of fact, they had aged synchronously with the persons who lived here, old Henry Reifsneider and his wife Phœbe Ann.

They had lived here, these two, ever since their marriage, forty-eight years before, and Henry had lived here before that from his childhood up. His father and mother, well along in years when he was a boy, had invited him to bring his wife here when he had first fallen in love and decided to marry; and he had done so. His father and mother were the companions of himself and his wife for ten years after they were married, when both died; and then Henry and Phœbe were left with their five children growing lustily apace. But all sorts of things had happened since then. Of the seven children, all told, that had been born to them, three had died; one girl had gone to Kansas; one boy had gone to Sioux Falls, never even to be heard of after; another boy had gone to Washington; and the last girl lived five counties away in the same State, but was so burdened with cares of her own that she rarely gave them a thought. Time and a commonplace home life that had never been attractive had weaned them thoroughly, so that, wherever they were, they gave little thought as to how it might be with their father and mother.

Old Henry Reifsneider and his wife Phœbe were a loving couple. You perhaps know how it is with simple natures that fasten themselves like lichens on the stones of circumstance and weather their days to a crumbling conclusion. The great world sounds widely, but it has no call for them. They have no soaring intellect. The orchard, the meadow, the corn-field, the pig-pen, and the chicken-lot measure the range of their human activities. When the wheat is headed it is reaped and threshed; when the corn is browned and frosted it is cut and shocked; when the timothy is in full head it is cut, and the hay-cock erected. After that comes winter, with the hauling of grain to market, the sawing and splitting of wood, the simple chores of fire-building, meal-getting, occasional repairing, and visiting. Beyond these and the changes of weather — the snows, the rains, and the fair days — there are no immediate, significant things. All the rest of life is a far-off, clamorous phantasmagoria, flickering like Northern lights in the night, and sounding as faintly as cow-bells tinkling in the distance.

Old Henry and his wife Phœbe were as fond of each other as it is possible for two old people to be who have nothing else in this life to be fond of. He was a thin old man, seventy when she died, a queer, crotchety person with coarse gray-black hair and beard, quite straggly and unkempt. He looked at you out of dull, fishy, watery eyes that had deep-brown crow's-feet at the sides. His clothes, like the clothes of many farmers, were aged and angular and baggy, standing out at the pockets, not fitting about the neck, protuberant and worn at elbow and knee. Phœbe Ann was thin and shapeless, a very umbrella of a woman, clad in shabby black, and with a black bonnet for her best wear. As time had passed, and they had only themselves to look after, their movements had become slower and slower, their activities fewer and fewer. The annual keep of pigs had been reduced from five to one grunting porker, and the single horse which Henry now retained was a sleepy animal, not over-nourished and not very clean. The chickens, of which formerly there was a large flock, had almost disappeared, owing to ferrets, foxes, and the lack of proper care, which produces disease. The former healthy garden was now a straggling memory of itself, and the vines and flower-beds that formerly ornamented the windows and dooryard had now become choking thickets. A will had been made which divided the small tax-eaten property equally among the remaining four, so that it was really of no interest to any of them. Yet these two lived together in peace and sympathy, only that now and then old Henry would become unduly cranky, complaining almost invariably that something had been neglected or mislaid which was of no importance at all.

"Phœbe, where's my corn-knife? You ain't never minded to let my things alone no more."

"Now you hush, Henry," his wife would caution him in a cracked and squeaky voice. "If you don't, I'll leave yuh. I'll git up and walk out of here some day, and then where would y' be? Y' ain't got anybody but me to look after yuh, so yuh just behave yourself. Your corn-knife's on the mantel where it's allus been unless you've gone an' put it summers else."

Old Henry, who knew his wife would never leave him in any circumstances, used to speculate at times as to what he would do if she were to die. That was the one leaving that he really feared. As he climbed on the chair at night to wind the old, long-pendulumed, double-weighted clock, or went finally to the front and the back door to see that they were safely shut in, it was a comfort to know that Phœbe was there, properly ensconced on her side of the bed, and that if he stirred restlessly in the night, she would be there to ask what he wanted.

"Now, Henry, do lie still! You're as restless as a chicken."

"Well, I can't sleep, Phœbe."

"Well, yuh needn't roll so, anyhow. Yuh kin let me sleep."

This usually reduced him to a state of somnolent ease. If she wanted a pail of water, it was a grumbling pleasure for him to get it; and if she did rise first to build the fires, he saw that the wood was cut and placed within easy reach. They divided this simple world nicely between them.

As the years had gone on, however, fewer and fewer people had called. They were well-known for a distance of as much as ten square miles as old Mr. and Mrs. Reifsneider, honest, moderately Christian, but too old to be really interesting any longer. The writing of letters had become an almost impossible burden too difficult to continue or even negotiate via others, although an occasional letter still did arrive from the daughter in Pemberton County. Now and then some old friend stopped with a pie or cake or a roasted chicken or duck, or merely to see that they were well; but even these kindly minded visits were no longer frequent.

One day in the early spring of her sixty-fourth year Mrs. Reifsneider took sick, and from a low fever passed into some indefinable ailment which, because of her age, was no longer curable. Old Henry drove to Swinnerton, the neighboring town, and procured a doctor. Some friends called, and the immediate care of her was taken off his hands. Then one chill spring night she died, and old Henry, in a fog of sorrow and uncertainty, followed her body to the nearest graveyard, an unattractive space with a few pines growing in it. Although he might have gone to the daughter in Pemberton or sent for her, it was really too much trouble and he was too weary and fixed. It was suggested to him at once by one friend and another that he come to stay with them awhile, but he did not see fit. He was so old and so fixed in his notions and so accustomed to the exact surroundings he had known all his days, that he could not think of leaving. He wanted to remain near where they had put his Phœbe; and the fact that he would have to live alone did not trouble him in the least. The living children were notified and the care of him offered if he would leave, but he would not.

"I kin make a shift for myself," he continually announced to old Dr. Morrow, who had attended his wife in this case. "I kin cook a little, and, besides, it don't take much more'n coffee an' bread in the mornin's to satisfy me. I'll get along now well enough. Yuh just let me be." And after many pleadings and proffers of advice, with supplies of coffee and bacon and baked bread duly offered and accepted, he was left to himself. For a while he sat idly outside his door brooding in the spring sun. He tried to revive his interest in farming, and to keep himself busy and free from thought by looking after the fields, which of late had been much neglected. It was a gloomy thing to come in of an evening, however, or in the afternoon and find no shadow of Phœbe where everything suggested her. By degrees he put a few of her things away. At night he sat beside his lamp and read in the papers that were left him occasionally or in a Bible that he had neglected for years, but he could get little solace from these things. Mostly he held his hand over his mouth and looked at the floor as he sat and thought of what had become of her, and how soon he himself would die. He made a great business of making his coffee in the morning and frying himself a little bacon at night; but his appetite was gone. The shell in which he had been housed so long seemed vacant, and its shadows were suggestive of immedicable griefs. So he lived quite dolefully for five long months, and then a change began.

It was one night, after he had looked after the front and the back door, wound the clock, blown out the light, and gone through all the selfsame motions that he had indulged in for years, that he went to bed not so much to sleep as to think. It was a moonlight night. The green-lichen-covered orchard just outside and to be seen from his bed where he now lay was a silvery affair, sweetly spectral. The moon shone through the east windows, throwing the pattern of the panes on the wooden floor, and making the old furniture, to which he was accustomed, stand out dimly in the room. As usual he had been thinking of Phœbe and the years when they had been young together, and of the children who had gone, and the poor shift he was making of his present days. The house was coming to be in a very bad state indeed. The bed-clothes were in disorder and not clean, for he made a wretched shift of washing. It was a terror to him. The roof leaked, causing things, some of them, to remain damp for weeks at a time, but he was getting into that brooding state where he would accept anything rather than exert himself. He preferred to pace slowly to and fro or to sit and think.

By twelve o'clock of this particular night he was asleep, however, and by two had waked again. The moon by this time had shifted to a position on the western side of the house, and it now shone in through the windows of the living-room and those of the kitchen beyond. A certain combination of furniture — a chair near a table, with his coat on it, the half-open kitchen door casting a shadow, and the position of a lamp near a paper — gave him an exact representation of Phœbe leaning over the table as he had often seen her do in life. It gave him a great start. Could it be she — or her ghost? He had scarcely ever believed in spirits; and still —— He looked at her fixedly in the feeble half-light, his old hair tingling oddly at the roots, and then sat up. The figure did not move. He put his thin legs out of the bed and sat looking at her, wondering if this could really be Phœbe. They had talked of ghosts often in their lifetime, of apparitions and omens; but they had never agreed that such things could be. It had never been a part of his wife's creed that she could have a spirit that could return to walk the earth. Her after-world was quite a different affair, a vague heaven, no less, from which the righteous did not trouble to return. Yet here she was now, bending over the table in her black skirt and gray shawl, her pale profile outlined against the moonlight.

"Phœbe," he called, thrilling from head to toe and putting out one bony hand, "have yuh come back?"

The figure did not stir, and he arose and walked uncertainly to the door, looking at it fixedly the while. As he drew near, however, the apparition resolved itself into its primal content — his old coat over the high-backed chair, the lamp by the paper, the half-open door.

"Well," he said to himself, his mouth open, "I thought shore I saw her." And he ran his hand strangely and vaguely through his hair, the while his nervous tension relaxed. Vanished as it had, it gave him the idea that she might return.

Another night, because of this first illusion, and because his mind was now constantly on her and he was old, he looked out of the window that was nearest his bed and commanded a hen-coop and pig-pen and a part of the wagon-shed, and there, a faint mist exuding from the damp of the ground, he thought he saw her again. It was one of those little wisps of mist, one of those faint exhalations of the earth that rise in a cool night after a warm day, and flicker like small white cypresses of fog before they disappear. In life it had been a custom of hers to cross this lot from her kitchen door to the pig-pen to throw in any scrap that was left from her cooking, and here she was again. He sat up and watched it strangely, doubtfully, because of his previous experience, but inclined, because of the nervous titillation that passed over his body, to believe that spirits really were, and that Phœbe, who would be concerned because of his lonely state, must be thinking about him, and hence returning. What other way would she have? How otherwise could she express herself? It would be within the province of her charity so to do, and like her loving interest in him. He quivered and watched it eagerly; but, a faint breath of air stirring, it wound away toward the fence and disappeared.

A third night, as he was actually dreaming, some ten days later, she came to his bedside and put her hand on his head.

"Poor Henry!" she said. "It's too bad."

He roused out of his sleep, actually to see her, he thought, moving from his bed-room into the one living-room, her figure a shadowy mass of black. The weak straining of his eyes caused little points of light to flicker about the outlines of her form. He arose, greatly astonished, walked the floor in the cool room, convinced that Phœbe was coming back to him. If he only thought sufficiently, if he made it perfectly clear by his feeling that he needed her greatly, she would come back, this kindly wife, and tell him what to do. She would perhaps be with him much of the time, in the night, anyhow; and that would make him less lonely, this state more endurable.

In age and with the feeble it is not such a far cry from the subtleties of illusion to actual hallucination, and in due time this transition was made for Henry. Night after night he waited, expecting her return. Once in his weird mood he thought he saw a pale light moving about the room, and another time he thought he saw her walking in the orchard after dark. It was one morning when the details of his lonely state were virtually unendurable that he woke with the thought that she was not dead. How he had arrived at this conclusion it is hard to say. His mind had gone. In its place was a fixed illusion. He and Phœbe had had a senseless quarrel. He had reproached her for not leaving his pipe where he was accustomed to find it, and she had left. It was an aberrated fulfillment of her old jesting threat that if he did not behave himself she would leave him.

"I guess I could find yuh ag'in," he had always said. But her cackling threat had always been:

"Yuh'll not find me if I ever leave yuh. I guess I kin git some place where yuh can't find me."

This morning when he arose he did not think to build the fire in the customary way or to grind his coffee and cut his bread, as was his wont, but solely to meditate as to where he should search for her and how he should induce her to come back. Recently the one horse had been dispensed with because he found it cumbersome and beyond his needs. He took down his soft crush hat after he had dressed himself, a new glint of interest and determination in his eye, and taking his black crook cane from behind the door, where he had always placed it, started out briskly to look for her among the nearest neighbors. His old shoes clumped soundly in the dust as he walked, and his gray-black locks, now grown rather long, straggled out in a dramatic fringe or halo from under his hat. His short coat stirred busily as he walked, and his hands and face were peaked and pale.

"Why, hello, Henry! Where're yuh goin' this mornin'?" inquired Farmer Dodge, who, hauling a load of wheat to market, encountered him on the public road. He had not seen the aged farmer in months, not since his wife's death, and he wondered now, seeing him looking so spry.

"Yuh ain't seen Phœbe, have yuh?" inquired the old man, looking up quizzically.

"Phœbe who?" inquired Farmer Dodge, not for the moment connecting the name with Henry's dead wife.

"Why, my wife Phœbe, o' course. Who do yuh s'pose I mean?" He stared up with a pathetic sharpness of glance from under his shaggy, gray eyebrows.

"Wall, I'll swan, Henry, yuh ain't jokin', are yuh?" said the solid Dodge, a pursy man, with a smooth, hard, red face. "It can't be your wife yuh're talkin' about. She's dead."

"Dead! Shucks!" retorted the demented Reifsneider. "She left me early this mornin', while I was sleepin'. She allus got up to build the fire, but she's gone now. We had a little spat last night, an' I guess that's the reason. But I guess I kin find her. She's gone over to Matilda Race's; that's where she's gone."

He started briskly up the road, leaving the amazed Dodge to stare in wonder after him.

"Well, I'll be switched!" he said aloud to himself. "He's clean out'n his head. That poor old feller's been livin' down there till he's gone outen his mind. I'll have to notify the authorities." And he flicked his whip with great enthusiasm. "Geddap!" he said, and was off.

Reifsneider met no one else in this poorly populated region until he reached the whitewashed fence of Matilda Race and her husband three miles away. He had passed several other houses en route, but these not being within the range of his illusion were not considered. His wife, who had known Matilda well, must be here. He opened the picket-gate which guarded the walk, and stamped briskly up to the door.

"Why, Mr. Reifsneider," exclaimed old Matilda herself, a stout woman, looking out of the door in answer to his knock, "what brings yuh here this mornin'?"

"Is Phœbe here?" he demanded eagerly.

"Phœbe who? What Phœbe?" replied Mrs. Race, curious as to this sudden development of energy on his part.

"Why, my Phœbe, o' course. My wife Phœbe. Who do yuh s'pose? Ain't she here now?"

"Lawsy me!" exclaimed Mrs. Race, opening her mouth. "Yuh pore man! So you're clean out'n your mind now. Yuh come right in and sit down. I'll git yuh a cup o' coffee. O' course your wife ain't here; but yuh come in an' sit down. I'll find her fer yuh after a while. I know where she is."

The old farmer's eyes softened, and he entered. He was so thin and pale a specimen, pantalooned and patriarchal, that he aroused Mrs. Race's extremest sympathy as he took off his hat and laid it on his knees quite softly and mildly.

"We had a quarrel last night, an' she left me," he volunteered.

"Laws! laws!" sighed Mrs. Race, there being no one present with whom to share her astonishment as she went to her kitchen. "The pore man! Now somebody's just got to look after him. He can't be allowed to run around the country this way lookin' for his dead wife. It's turrible."

She boiled him a pot of coffee and brought in some of her new-baked bread and fresh butter. She set out some of her best jam and put a couple of eggs to boil, lying whole-heartedly the while.

"Now yuh stay right there, Uncle Henry, till Jake comes in, an' I'll send him to look for Phœbe. I think it's more'n likely she's over to Swinnerton with some o' her friends. Anyhow, we'll find out. Now yuh just drink this coffee an' eat this bread. Yuh must be tired. Yuh've had a long walk this mornin'." Her idea was to take counsel with Jake, "her man," and perhaps have him notify the authorities.

She bustled about, meditating on the uncertainties of life, while old Reifsneider thrummed on the rim of his hat with his pale fingers and later ate abstractedly of what she offered. His mind was on his wife, however, and since she was not here, or did not appear, it wandered vaguely away to a family by the name of Murray, miles away in another direction. He decided after a time that he would not wait for Jake Race to hunt his wife but would seek her for himself. He must be on, and urge her to come back.

"Well, I'll be goin'," he said, getting up and looking strangely about him. "I guess she didn't come here after all. She went over to the Murrays', I guess. I'll not wait any longer, Mis' Race. There's a lot to do over to the house to-day." And out he marched in the face of her protests taking to the dusty road again in the warm spring sun, his cane striking the earth as he went.

It was two hours later that this pale figure of a man appeared in the Murrays' doorway, dusty, perspiring, eager. He had tramped all of five miles, and it was noon. An amazed husband and wife of sixty heard his strange query, and realized also that he was mad. They begged him to stay to dinner, intending to notify the authorities later and see what could be done; but though he stayed to partake of a little something, he did not stay long, and was off again to another distant farmhouse, his idea of many things to do and his need of Phœbe impelling him. So it went for that day and the next and the next, the circle of his inquiry ever widening.

The process by which a character assumes the significance of being peculiar, his antics weird, yet harmless, in such a community is often involute and pathetic. This day, as has been said, saw Reifsneider at other doors, eagerly asking his unnatural question, and leaving a trail of amazement, sympathy, and pity in his wake. Although the authorities were informed — the county sheriff, no less — it was not deemed advisable to take him into custody; for when those who knew old Henry, and had for so long, reflected on the condition of the county insane asylum, a place which, because of the poverty of the district, was of staggering aberration and sickening environment, it was decided to let him remain at large; for, strange to relate, it was found on investigation that at night he returned peaceably enough to his lonesome domicile there to discover whether his wife had returned, and to brood in loneliness until the morning. Who would lock up a thin, eager, seeking old man with iron-gray hair and an attitude of kindly, innocent inquiry, particularly when he was well known for a past of only kindly servitude and reliability? Those who had known him best rather agreed that he should be allowed to roam at large. He could do no harm. There were many who were willing to help him as to food, old clothes, the odds and ends of his daily life — at least at first. His figure after a time became not so much a common-place as an accepted curiosity, and the replies, "Why, no, Henry; I ain't see her," or "No, Henry; she ain't been here to-day," more customary.

For several years thereafter then he was an odd figure in the sun and rain, on dusty roads and muddy ones, encountered occasionally in strange and unexpected places, pursuing his endless search. Undernourishment, after a time, although the neighbors and those who knew his history gladly contributed from their store, affected his body; for he walked much and ate little. The longer he roamed the public highway in this manner, the deeper became his strange hallucination; and finding it harder and harder to return from his more and more distant pilgrimages, he finally began taking a few utensils with him from his home, making a small package of them, in order that he might not be compelled to return. In an old tin coffee-pot of large size he placed a small tin cup, a knife, fork, and spoon, some salt and pepper, and to the outside of it, by a string forced through a pierced hole, he fastened a plate, which could be released, and which was his woodland table. It was no trouble for him to secure the little food that he needed, and with a strange, almost religious dignity, he had no hesitation in asking for that much. By degrees his hair became longer and longer, his once black hat became an earthen brown, and his clothes threadbare and dusty.

For all of three years he walked, and none knew how wide were his perambulations, nor how he survived the storms and cold. They could not see him, with homely rural understanding and forethought, sheltering himself in hay-cocks, or by the sides of cattle, whose warm bodies protected him from the cold, and whose dull understandings were not opposed to his harmless presence. Overhanging rocks and trees kept him at times from the rain, and a friendly hay-loft or corn-crib was not above his humble consideration.

The involute progression of hallucination is strange. From asking at doors and being constantly rebuffed or denied, he finally came to the conclusion that although his Phœbe might not be in any of the houses at the doors of which he inquired, she might nevertheless be within the sound of his voice. And so, from patient inquiry, he began to call sad, occasional cries, that ever and anon waked the quiet landscapes and ragged hill regions, and set to echoing his thin "O-o-o Phœbe! O-o-o Phœbe!" It had a pathetic, albeit insane, ring, and many a farmer or plowboy came to know it even from afar and say, "There goes old Reifsneider."

Another thing that puzzled him greatly after a time and after many hundreds of inquiries was, when he no longer had any particular dooryard in view and no special inquiry to make, which way to go. These cross-roads, which occasionally led in four or even six directions, came after a time to puzzle him. But to solve this knotty problem, which became more and more of a puzzle, there came to his aid another hallucination. Phœbe's spirit or some power of the air or wind or nature would tell him. If he stood at the center of the parting of the ways, closed his eyes, turned thrice about, and called "O-o-o Phœbe!" twice, and then threw his cane straight before him, that would surely indicate which way to go for Phœbe, or one of these mystic powers would surely govern its direction and fall! In whichever direction it went, even though, as was not infrequently the case, it took him back along the path he had already come, or across fields, he was not so far gone in his mind but that he gave himself ample time to search before he called again. Also the hallucination seemed to persist that at some time he would surely find her. There were hours when his feet were sore, and his limbs weary, when he would stop in the heat to wipe his seamed brow, or in the cold to beat his arms. Sometimes, after throwing away his cane, and finding it indicating the direction from which he had just come, he would shake his head wearily and philosophically, as if contemplating the unbelievable or an untoward fate, and then start briskly off. His strange figure came finally to be known in the farthest reaches of three or four counties. Old Reifsneider was a pathetic character. His fame was wide.

Near a little town called Watersville, in Green County, perhaps four miles from that minor center of human activity, there was a place or precipice locally known as the Red Cliff, a sheer wall of red sandstone, perhaps a hundred feet high, which raised its sharp face for half a mile or more above the fruitful corn-fields and orchards that lay beneath, and which was surmounted by a thick grove of trees. The slope that slowly led up to it from the opposite side was covered by a rank growth of beech, hickory, and ash, through which threaded a number of wagon-tracks crossing at various angles. In fair weather it had become old Reifsneider's habit, so inured was he by now to the open, to make his bed in some such patch of trees as this to fry his bacon or boil his eggs at the foot of some tree before laying himself down for the night. Occasionally, so light and inconsequential was his sleep, he would walk at night. More often, the moonlight or some sudden wind stirring in the trees or a reconnoitering animal arousing him, he would sit up and think, or pursue his quest in the moonlight or the dark, a strange, unnatural, half wild, half savage-looking but utterly harmless creature, calling at lonely road crossings, staring at dark and shuttered houses, and wondering where, where Phœbe could really be.

That particular lull that comes in the systole-diastole of this earthly ball at two o'clock in the morning invariably aroused him, and though he might not go any farther he would sit up and contemplate the darkness or the stars, wondering. Sometimes in the strange processes of his mind he would fancy that he saw moving among the trees the figure of his lost wife, and then he would get up to follow, taking his utensils, always on a string, and his cane. If she seemed to evade him too easily he would run, or plead, or, suddenly losing track of the fancied figure, stand awed or disappointed, grieving for the moment over the almost insurmountable difficulties of his search.

It was in the seventh year of these hopeless peregrinations, in the dawn of a similar springtime to that in which his wife had died, that he came at last one night to the vicinity of this self-same patch that crowned the rise to the Red Cliff. His far-flung cane, used as a divining-rod at the last cross-roads, had brought him hither. He had walked many, many miles. It was after ten o'clock at night, and he was very weary. Long wandering and little eating had left him but a shadow of his former self. It was a question now not so much of physical strength but of spiritual endurance which kept him up. He had scarcely eaten this day, and now exhausted he set himself down in the dark to rest and possibly to sleep.

Curiously on this occasion a strange suggestion of the presence of his wife surrounded him. It would not be long now, he counseled with himself, although the long months had brought him nothing, until he should see her, talk to her. He fell asleep after a time, his head on his knees. At midnight the moon began to rise, and at two in the morning, his wakeful hour, was a large silver disk shining through the trees to the east. He opened his eyes when the radiance became strong, making a silver pattern at his feet and lighting the woods with strange lusters and silvery, shadowy forms. As usual, his old notion that his wife must be near occurred to him on this occasion, and he looked about him with a speculative, anticipatory eye. What was it that moved in the distant shadows along the path by which he had entered — a pale, flickering will-o'-the-wisp that bobbed gracefully among the trees and riveted his expectant gaze? Moonlight and shadows combined to give it a strange form and a stranger reality, this fluttering of bog-fire or dancing of wandering fire-flies. Was it truly his lost Phœbe? By a circuitous route it passed about him, and in his fevered state he fancied that he could see the very eyes of her, not as she was when he last saw her in the black dress and shawl but now a strangely younger Phœbe, gayer, sweeter, the one whom he had known years before as a girl. Old Reifsneider got up. He had been expecting and dreaming of this hour all these years, and now as he saw the feeble light dancing lightly before him he peered at it questioningly, one thin hand in his gray hair.

Of a sudden there came to him now for the first time in many years the full charm of her girlish figure as he had known it in boyhood, the pleasing, sympathetic smile, the brown hair, the blue sash she had once worn about her waist at a picnic, her gay, graceful movements. He walked around the base of the tree, straining with his eyes, forgetting for once his cane and utensils, and following eagerly after. On she moved before him, a will-o'-the-wisp of the spring, a little flame above her head, and it seemed as though among the small saplings of ash and beech and the thick trunks of hickory and elm that she signaled with a young, a lightsome hand.

"O Phœbe! Phœbe!" he called. "Have yuh really come? Have yuh really answered me?" And hurrying faster, he fell once, scrambling lamely to his feet, only to see the light in the distance dancing illusively on. On and on he hurried until he was fairly running, brushing his ragged arms against the trees, striking his hands and face against impeding twigs. His hat was gone, his lungs were breathless, his reason quite astray, when coming to the edge of the cliff he saw her below among a silvery bed of apple-trees now blooming in the spring.

"O Phœbe!" he called. "O Phœbe! Oh, no, don't leave me!" And feeling the lure of a world where love was young and Phœbe as this vision presented her, a delightful epitome of their quondam youth, he gave a gay cry of "Oh, wait, Phœbe!" and leaped.

Some farmer-boys, reconnoitering this region of bounty and prospect some few days afterward, found first the tin utensils tied together under the tree where he had left them, and then later at the foot of the cliff, pale, broken, but elate, a molded smile of peace and delight upon his lips, his body. His old hat was discovered lying under some low-growing saplings the twigs of which had held it back. No one of all the simple population knew how eagerly and joyously he had found his lost mate.

The Second Choice[1]

SHIRLEY DEAR:

You don't want the letters. There are only six of them, anyhow, and think, they're all I have of you to cheer me on my travels. What good would they be to you — little bits of notes telling me you're sure to meet me — but me — think of me! If I send them to you, you'll tear them up, whereas if you leave them with me I can dab them with musk and ambergris and keep them in a little silver box, always beside me.

Ah, Shirley dear, you really don't know how sweet I think you are, how dear! There isn't a thing we have ever done together that isn't as clear in my mind as this great big skyscraper over the way here in Pittsburgh, and far more pleasing. In fact, my thoughts of you are the most precious and delicious things I have, Shirley.

But I'm too young to marry now. You know that, Shirley, don't you? I haven't placed myself in any way yet, and I'm so restless that I don't know whether I ever will, really. Only yesterday, old Roxbaum — that's my new employer here — came to me and wanted to know if I would like an assistant overseership on one of his coffee plantations in Java, said there would not be much money in it for a year or two, a bare living, but later there would be more — and I jumped at it. Just the thought of Java and going there did that, although I knew I could make more staying right here. Can't you see how it is with me, Shirl? I'm too restless and too young. I couldn't take care of you right, and you wouldn't like me after a while if I didn't.

But ah, Shirley sweet, I think the dearest things of you! There isn't an hour, it seems, but some little bit of you comes back — a dear, sweet bit — the night we sat on the grass in Tregore Park and counted the stars through the trees; that first evening at Sparrows Point when we missed the last train and had to walk to Langley. Remember the tree-toads, Shirl? And then that warm April Sunday in Atholby woods! Ah, Shirl, you don't want the six notes! Let me keep them.

---

1. "The Second Choice" first appeared in *Cosmopolitan*, February 1918 as "Second Choice."

But think of me, will you, sweet, wherever you go and whatever you do? I'll always think of you, and wish that you had met a better, saner man than me, and that I really could have married you and been all you wanted me to be. By-by, sweet. I may start for Java within the month. If so, and you would want them, I'll send you some cards from there — if they have any.

Your worthless,
ARTHUR.

She sat and turned the letter in her hand, dumb with despair. It was the very last letter she would ever get from him. Of that she was certain. He was gone now, once and for all. She had written him only once, not making an open plea but asking him to return her letters, and then there had come this tender but evasive reply, saying nothing of a possible return but desiring to keep her letters for old times' sake — the happy hours they had spent together.

The happy hours! Oh, yes, yes, yes — the happy hours!

In her memory now, as she sat here in her home after the day's work, meditating on all that had been in the few short months since he had come and gone, was a world of color and light — a color and a light so transfiguring as to seem celestial, but now, alas, wholly dissipated. It had contained so much of all she had desired — love, romance, amusement, laughter. He had been so gay and thoughtless, or headstrong, so youthfully romantic, and with such a love of play and change and to be saying and doing anything and everything. Arthur could dance in a gay way, whistle, sing after a fashion, play. He could play cards and do tricks, and he had such a superior air, so genial and brisk, with a kind of innate courtesy in it and yet an intolerance for slowness and stodginess or anything dull or dingy, such as characterized —— But here her thoughts fled from him. She refused to think of any one but Arthur.

Sitting in her little bedroom now, off the parlor on the ground floor in her home in Bethune Street, and looking out over the Kessels' yard, and beyond that — there being no fences in Bethune Street — over the "yards" or lawns of the Pollards, Bakers, Cryders, and others, she thought of how dull it must all have seemed to him, with his fine imaginative mind and experiences, his love of change and gayety, his atmosphere of something better than she had ever known. How little she had been fitted, perhaps, by beauty or temperament to overcome this — the something — dullness in her work or her home, which possibly had driven him away. For, although many had admired her to date, and she was young and pretty in her simple way and constantly receiving suggestions that her beauty was disturbing to some, still, he had not cared for her — he had gone.

And now, as she meditated, it seemed that this scene, and all that it stood for — her parents, her work, her daily shuttling to and fro between the drug company for which she worked and this street and house — was typical of her life and what she was destined to endure always. Some girls were so much more fortunate. They had fine clothes, fine homes, a world of pleasure and opportunity in which to move. They did not have to scrimp and save and work to pay their own way. And yet she had always been compelled to do it, but had never complained until now — or until he came, and after. Bethune Street, with its commonplace front yards and houses nearly all alike, and this house, so like the others, room for room and porch for porch, and her parents, too, really like all the others, had seemed good enough, quite satisfactory, indeed, until then. But now, now!

Here, in their kitchen, was her mother, a thin, pale, but kindly woman, peeling potatoes and washing lettuce, and putting a bit of steak or a chop or a piece of liver in a frying-pan day after day, morning and evening, month after month, year after year. And next door was Mrs. Kessel doing the same thing. And next door Mrs. Cryder. And next door Mrs. Pollard. But, until now, she had not thought it so bad. But now — now — oh! And on all the porches or lawns all along this street were the husbands and fathers, mostly middle-aged or old men like her father, reading their papers or cutting the grass before dinner, or smoking and meditating afterward. Her father was out in front now, a stooped, for-bearing, meditative soul, who had rarely anything to say — leaving it all to his wife, her mother, but who was fond of her in his dull, quiet way. He was a pattern-maker by trade, and had come into possession of this small, ordinary home via years of toil and saving, her mother helping him. They had no particular religion, as he often said, thinking reason-ably human conduct a sufficient passport to heaven, but they had gone occasionally to the Methodist Church over in Nicholas Street, and she had once joined it. But of late she had not gone, weaned away by the other commonplace pleasures of her world.

And then in the midst of it, the dull drift of things, as she now saw them to be, he had come — Arthur Bristow — young, energetic, good-looking, ambitious, dreamful, and instanter, and with her never know-ing quite how, the whole thing had been changed. He had appeared so swiftly — out of nothing, as it were.

Previous to him had been Barton Williams, stout, phlegmatic, good-natured, well-meaning, who was, or had been before Arthur came, asking her to marry him, and whom she allowed to half assume that she would.

She had liked him in a feeble, albeit, as she thought, tender way, thinking him the kind, according to the logic of her neighborhood, who would make her a good husband, and, until Arthur appeared on the scene, had really intended to marry him. It was not really a love-match, as she saw now, but she thought it was, which was much the same thing, perhaps. But, as she now recalled, when Arthur came, how the scales fell from her eyes! In a trice, as it were, nearly, there was a new heaven and a new earth. Arthur had arrived, and with him a sense of something different.

Mabel Gove had asked her to come over to her house in Westleigh, the adjoining suburb, for Thanksgiving eve and day, and without a thought of anything, and because Barton was busy handling a part of the work in the despatcher's office of the Great Eastern and could not see her, she had gone. And then, to her surprise and strange, almost ineffable delight, the moment she had seen him, he was there — Arthur, with his slim, straight figure and dark hair and eyes and clean-cut features, as clean and attractive as those of a coin. And as he had looked at her and smiled and narrated humorous bits of things that had happened to him, something had come over her — a spell — and after dinner they had all gone round to Edith Barringer's to dance, and there as she had danced with him, somehow, without any seeming boldness on his part, he had taken possession of her, as it were, drawn her close, and told her she had beautiful eyes and hair and such a delicately rounded chin, and that he thought she danced gracefully and was sweet. She had nearly fainted with delight.

"Do you like me?" he had asked in one place in the dance, and, in spite of herself, she had looked up into his eyes, and from that moment she was almost mad over him, could think of nothing else but his hair and eyes and his smile and his graceful figure.

Mabel Gove had seen it all, in spite of her determination that no one should, and on their going to bed later, back at Mabel's home, she had whispered:

"Ah, Shirley, I saw. You like Arthur, don't you?"

"I think he's very nice," Shirley recalled replying, for Mabel knew of her affair with Barton and liked him, "but I'm not crazy over him." And for this bit of treason she had sighed in her dreams nearly all night.

And the next day, true to a request and a promise made by him, Arthur had called again at Mabel's to take her and Mabel to a "movie" which was not so far away, and from there they had gone to an ice-cream parlor, and during it all, when Mabel was not looking, he had squeezed her arm and hand and kissed her neck, and she had held her breath, and her heart had seemed to stop.

"And now you're going to let me come out to your place to see you, aren't you?" he had whispered.

And she had replied, "Wednesday evening," and then written the address on a little piece of paper and given it to him.

But now it was all gone, gone!

This house, which now looked so dreary — how romantic it had seemed that first night *he* called — the front room with its commonplace furniture, and later in the spring, the veranda, with its vines just sprouting, and the moon in May. Oh, the moon in May, and June and July, when he was here! How she had lied to Barton to make evenings for Arthur, and occasionally to Arthur to keep him from contact with Barton. She had not even mentioned Barton to Arthur because — because — well, because Arthur was so much better, and somehow (she admitted it to herself now) she had not been sure that Arthur would care for her long, if at all, and then — well, and then, to be quite frank, Barton might be good enough. She did not exactly hate him because she had found Arthur — not at all. She still liked him in a way — he was so kind and faithful, so very dull and straightforward and thoughtful of her, which Arthur was certainly not. Before Arthur had appeared, as she well remembered, Barton had seemed to be plenty good enough — in fact, all that she desired in a pleasant, companionable way, calling for her, taking her places, bringing her flowers and candy, which Arthur rarely did, and for that, if nothing more, she could not help continuing to like him and to feel sorry for him, and, besides, as she had admitted to herself before, if Arthur left her — * * * * * Weren't his parents better off than hers — and hadn't he a good position for such a man as he — one hundred and fifty dollars a month and the certainty of more later on? A little while before meeting Arthur, she had thought this very good, enough for two to live on at least, and she had thought some of trying it at some time or other — but now — now —

And that first night he had called — how well she remembered it — how it had transfigured the parlor next this in which she was now, filling it with something it had never had before, and the porch outside, too, for that matter, with its gaunt, leafless vine, and this street, too, even — dull, commonplace Bethune Street. There had been a flurry of snow during the afternoon while she was working at the store, and the ground was white with it. All the neighboring homes seemed to look sweeter and happier and more inviting than ever they had as she came past them, with their lights peeping from under curtains and drawn shades. She had hurried into hers and lighted the big red-shaded parlor lamp, her one artistic treasure, as she thought, and put it near the piano, between it and the window, and arranged the chairs, and then bustled to the task of making herself as pleasing as she might. For him she had gotten out her one best filmy house dress and done up her hair in the fashion she thought most becoming — and that he had not seen before — and powdered her cheeks and nose and darkened her eyelashes, as some of the girls at the store did, and put on her new gray satin slippers, and then, being so arrayed, waited nervously, unable to eat anything or to think of anything but him.

And at last, just when she had begun to think he might not be coming, he had appeared with that arch smile and a "Hello! It's here you live, is it? I was wondering. George, but you're twice as sweet as I thought you were, aren't you?" And then, in the little entryway, behind the closed door, he had held her and kissed her on the mouth a dozen times while she pretended to push against his coat and struggle and say that her parents might hear.

And, oh, the room afterward, with him in it in the red glow of the lamp, and with his pale handsome face made handsomer thereby, as she thought! He had made her sit near him and had held her hands and told her about his work and his dreams — all that he expected to do in the future — and then she had found herself wishing intensely to share just such a life — his life — anything that he might wish to do; only, she kept wondering, with a slight pain, whether he would want her to — he was so young, dreamful, ambitious, much younger and more dreamful than herself, although, in reality, he was several years older.

And then followed that glorious period from December to this late September, in which everything which was worth happening in love had happened. Oh, those wondrous days the following spring, when, with the first burst of buds and leaves, he had taken her one Sunday to Atholby, where all the great woods were, and they had hunted spring beauties in the grass, and sat on a slope and looked at the river below and watched some boys fixing up a sailboat and setting forth in it quite as she wished she and Arthur might be doing — going somewhere together — far, far away from all commonplace things and life! And then he had slipped his arm about her and kissed her cheek and neck, and tweaked her ear and smoothed her hair — and oh, there on the grass, with the spring flowers about her and a canopy of small green leaves above, the perfection of love had come — love so wonderful that the mere thought of it made her eyes brim now! And then had been days, Saturday afternoons and Sundays, at Atholby and Sparrows Point, where the great beach was, and in lovely Tregore Park, a mile or two from her home, where they could go of an evening and sit in or near the pavilion and have ice-cream and dance or watch the dancers. Oh, the stars, the winds, the summer breath of those days! Ah, me! Ah, me!

Naturally, her parents had wondered from the first about her and Arthur, and her and Barton, since Barton had already assumed a proprietary interest in her and she had seemed to like him. But then she was an only child and a pet, and used to presuming on that, and they could not think of saying anything to her. After all, she was young and pretty and was entitled to change her mind; only, only — she had had to indulge in a career of lying and subterfuge in connection with Barton, since Arthur was headstrong and wanted every evening that he chose — to call for her at the store and keep her down-town to dinner and a show.

Arthur had never been like Barton, shy, phlegmatic, obedient, waiting long and patiently for each little favor, but, instead, masterful and eager, rifling her of kisses and caresses and every delight of love, and teasing and playing with her as a cat would a mouse. She could never resist him. He demanded of her her time and her affection without let or hindrance. He was not exactly selfish or cruel, as some might have been, but gay and unthinking at times, unconsciously so, and yet loving and tender at others — nearly always so. But always he would talk of things in the future as if they really did not include her — and this troubled her greatly — of places he might go, things he might do, which, somehow, he seemed to think or assume that she could not or would not do with him. He was always going to Australia sometime, he thought, in a business way, or to South Africa, or possibly to India. He never seemed to have any fixed clear future for himself in mind.

A dreadful sense of helplessness and of impending disaster came over her at these times, of being involved in some predicament over which she had no control, and which would lead her on to some sad end. Arthur, although plainly in love, as she thought, and apparently delighted with her, might not always love her. She began, timidly at first (and always, for that matter), to ask him pretty, seeking questions about himself and her, whether their future was certain to be together, whether he really wanted her — loved her — whether he might not want to marry some one else or just her, and whether she wouldn't look nice in a pearl satin wedding-dress with a long creamy veil and satin slippers and a bouquet of bridal-wreath. She had been so slowly but surely saving to that end, even before he came, in connection with Barton; only, after *he* came, all thought of the import of it had been transferred to him. But now, also, she was beginning to ask herself sadly, "Would it ever be?" He was so airy, so inconsequential, so ready to say: "Yes, yes," and "Sure, sure! That's right! Yes, indeedy; you bet! Say, kiddie, but you'll look sweet!" but, somehow, it had always seemed as if this whole thing were a glorious interlude and that it could not last. Arthur was too gay and ethereal and too little settled in his own mind. His ideas of travel and living in different cities, finally winding up in New York or San Francisco, but never with her exactly until she asked him, was too ominous, although he always reassured her gaily: "Of course! Of course!" But somehow she could never believe it really, and it made her intensely sad at times, horribly gloomy. So often she wanted to cry, and she could scarcely tell why.

And then, because of her intense affection for him, she had finally quarreled with Barton, or nearly that, if one could say that one ever really quarreled with him. It had been because of a certain Thursday evening a few weeks before about which she had disappointed him. In a fit of generosity, knowing that Arthur was coming Wednesday, and because Barton had stopped in at the store to see her, she had told him that he might come, having regretted it afterward, so enamored was she of Arthur. And then when Wednesday came, Arthur had changed his mind, telling her he would come Friday instead, but on Thursday evening he had stopped in at the store and asked her to go to Sparrows Point, with the result that she had no time to notify Barton. He had gone to the house and sat with her parents until ten-thirty, and then, a few days later, although she had written him offering an excuse, had called at the store to complain slightly.

"Do you think you did just right, Shirley? You might have sent word, mightn't you? Who was it — the new fellow you won't tell me about?"

Shirley flared on the instant.

"Supposing it was? What's it to you? I don't belong to you yet, do I? I told you there wasn't any one, and I wish you'd let me alone about that. I couldn't help it last Thursday — that's all — and I don't want you to be fussing with me — that's all. If you don't want to, you needn't come any more, anyhow."

"Don't say that, Shirley," pleaded Barton. "You don't mean that. I won't bother you, though, if you don't want me any more."

And because Shirley sulked, not knowing what else to do, he had gone and she had not seen him since.

And then sometime later when she had thus broken with Barton, avoiding the railway station where he worked, Arthur had failed to come at his appointed time, sending no word until the next day, when a note came to the store saying that he had been out of town for his firm over Sunday and had not been able to notify her, but that he would call Tuesday. It was an awful blow. At the time, Shirley had a vision of what was to follow. It seemed for the moment as if the whole world had suddenly been reduced to ashes, that there was nothing but black charred cinders anywhere — she felt that about all life. Yet it all came to her clearly then that this was but the beginning of just such days and just such excuses, and that soon, soon, he would come no more. He was beginning to be tired of her and soon he would not even make excuses. She felt it, and it froze and terrified her.

And then, soon after, the indifference which she feared did follow —
almost created by her own thoughts, as it were. First, it was a meeting he
had to attend somewhere one Wednesday night when he was to have
come for her. Then he was going out of town again, over Sunday. Then
he was going away for a whole week — it was absolutely unavoidable, he
said, his commercial duties were increasing — and once he had casually
remarked that nothing could stand in the way where she was
concerned — never! She did not think of reproaching him with this; she
was too proud. If he was going, he must go. She would not be willing to
say to herself that she had ever attempted to hold any man. But, just the
same, she was agonized by the thought. When he was with her, he
seemed tender enough; only, at times, his eyes wandered and he seemed
slightly bored. Other girls, particularly pretty ones, seemed to interest
him as much as she did.

And the agony of the long days when he did not come any more for a
week or two at a time! The waiting, the brooding, the wondering, at the
store and here in her home — in the former place making mistakes at
times because she could not get her mind off him and being reminded
of them, and here at her own home at nights, being so absent-minded
that her parents remarked on it. She felt sure that her parents must be
noticing that Arthur was not coming any more, or as much as he had —
for she pretended to be going out with him, going to Mabel Gove's
instead — and that Barton had deserted her too, he having been driven
off by her indifference, never to come any more, perhaps, unless she
sought him out.

And then it was that the thought of saving her own face by taking up
with Barton once more occurred to her, of using him and his affections
and faithfulness and dulness, if you will, to cover up her own dilemma.
Only, this ruse was not to be tried until she had written Arthur this one
letter — a pretext merely to see if there was a single ray of hope, a letter to
be written in a gentle-enough way and asking for the return of the few
notes she had written him. She had not seen him now in nearly a
month, and the last time she had, he had said he might soon be
compelled to leave her awhile — to go to Pittsburgh to work. And it was
his reply to this that she now held in her hand — from Pittsburgh! It was
frightful! The future without him!

But Barton would never know really what had transpired, if she went
back to him. In spite of all her delicious hours with Arthur, she could
call him back, she felt sure. She had never really entirely dropped him,
and he knew it. He had bored her dreadfully on occasion, arriving on off
days when Arthur was not about, with flowers or candy, or both, and
sitting on the porch steps and talking of the railroad business and of the

whereabouts and doings of some of their old friends. It was shameful, she had thought at times, to see a man so patient, so hopeful, so good-natured as Barton, deceived in this way, and by her, who was so miserable over another. Her parents must see and know, she had thought at these times, but still, what else was she to do?

"I'm a bad girl," she kept telling herself. "I'm all wrong. What right have I to offer Barton what is left?" But still, somehow, she realized that Barton, if she chose to favor him, would only be too grateful for even the leavings of others where she was concerned, and that even yet, if she but deigned to crook a finger, she could have him. He was so simple, so good-natured, so stolid and matter of fact, so different to Arthur whom (she could not help smiling at the thought of it) she was loving now about as Barton loved her — slavishly, hopelessly.

And then, as the days passed and Arthur did not write any more — just this one brief note — she at first grieved horribly, and then in a fit of numb despair attempted, bravely enough from one point of view, to adjust herself to the new situation. Why should she despair? Why die of agony where there were plenty who would still sigh for her — Barton among others? She was young, pretty, very — many told her so. She could, if she chose, achieve a vivacity which she did not feel. Why should she brook this unkindness without a thought of retaliation? Why shouldn't she enter upon a gay and heartless career, indulging in a dozen flirtations at once — dancing and killing all thoughts of Arthur in a round of frivolities? There were many who beckoned to her. She stood at her counter in the drug store on many a day and brooded over this, but at the thought of which one to begin with, she faltered. After her late love, all were so tame, for the present anyhow.

And then — and then — always there was Barton, the humble or faithful, to whom she had been so unkind and whom she had used and whom she still really liked. So often self-reproaching thoughts in connection with him crept over her. He must have known, must have seen how badly she was using him all this while, and yet he had not failed to come and come, until she had actually quarreled with him, and any one would have seen that it was literally hopeless. She could not help remembering, especially now in her pain, that he adored her. He was not calling on her now at all — by her indifference she had finally driven him away — but a word, a word — She waited for days, weeks, hoping against hope, and then ——

The office of Barton's superior in the Great Eastern terminal had always made him an easy object for her blandishments, coming and going, as she frequently did, via this very station. He was in the office of the assistant train-despatcher on the ground floor, where passing to and from the local, which, at times, was quicker than a street-car, she could easily see him by peering in; only, she had carefully avoided him for nearly a year. If she chose now, and would call for a message-blank at the adjacent telegraph-window which was a part of his room, and raised her voice as she often had in the past, he could scarcely fail to hear, if he did not see her. And if he did, he would rise and come over — of that she was sure, for he never could resist her. It had been a wile of hers in the old days to do this or to make her presence felt by idling outside. After a month of brooding, she felt that she must act — her position as a deserted girl was too much. She could not stand it any longer really — the eyes of her mother, for one.

It was six-fifteen one evening when, coming out of the store in which she worked, she turned her step disconsolately homeward. Her heart was heavy, her face rather pale and drawn. She had stopped in the store's retiring-room before coming out to add to her charms as much as possible by a little powder and rouge and to smooth her hair. It would not take much to reallure her former sweetheart, she felt sure — and yet it might not be so easy after all. Suppose he had found another? But she could not believe that. It had scarcely been long enough since he had last attempted to see her, and he was really so very, very fond of her and so faithful. He was too slow and certain in his choosing — he had been so with her. Still, who knows? With this thought, she went forward in the evening, feeling for the first time the shame and pain that comes of deception, the agony of having to relinquish an ideal and the feeling of despair that comes to those who find themselves in the position of suppliants, stooping to something which in better days and better fortune they would not know. Arthur was the cause of this.

When she reached the station, the crowd that usually filled it at this hour was swarming. There were so many pairs like Arthur and herself laughing and hurrying away or so she felt. First glancing in the small mirror of a weighing scale to see if she were still of her former charm, she stopped thoughtfully at a little flower stand which stood outside, and for a few pennies purchased a tiny bunch of violets. She then went inside and stood near the window, peering first furtively to see if he were present. He was. Bent over his work, a green shade over his eyes, she could see his stolid, genial figure at a table. Stepping back a moment to ponder, she finally went forward and, in a clear voice, asked,

"May I have a blank, please?"

The infatuation of the discarded Barton was such that it brought him instantly to his feet. In his stodgy, stocky way he rose, his eyes glowing with a friendly hope, his mouth wreathed in smiles, and came over. At the sight of her, pale, but pretty — paler and prettier, really, than he had ever seen her — he thrilled dumbly.

"How are you, Shirley?" he asked sweetly, as he drew near, his eyes searching her face hopefully. He had not seen her for so long that he was intensely hungry, and her paler beauty appealed to him more than ever. Why wouldn't she have him? he was asking himself. Why wouldn't his persistent love yet win her? Perhaps it might. "I haven't seen you in a month of Sundays, it seems. How are the folks?"

"They're all right, Bart," she smiled archly, "and so am I. How have you been? It has been a long time since I've seen you. I've been wondering how you were. Have you been all right? I was just going to send a message."

As he had approached, Shirley had pretended at first not to see him, a moment later to affect surprise, although she was really suppressing a heavy sigh. The sight of him, after Arthur, was not reassuring. Could she really interest herself in him any more? Could she?

"Sure, sure," he replied genially; "I'm always all right. You couldn't kill me, you know. Not going away, are you, Shirl?" he queried interestedly.

"No; I'm just telegraphing to Mabel. She promised to meet me tomorrow, and I want to be sure she will."

"You don't come past here as often as you did, Shirley," he complained tenderly. "At least, I don't seem to see you so often," he added with a smile. "It isn't anything I have done, is it?" he queried, and then, when she protested quickly, added: "What's the trouble, Shirl? Haven't been sick, have you?"

She affected all her old gaiety and ease, feeling as though she would like to cry.

"Oh, no," she returned; "I've been all right. I've been going through the other door, I suppose, or coming in and going out on the Langdon Avenue car." (This was true, because she had been wanting to avoid him.) "I've been in such a hurry, most nights, that I haven't had time to stop, Bart. You know how late the store keeps us at times."

He remembered, too, that in the old days she had made time to stop or meet him occasionally.

"Yes, I know," he said tactfully. "But you haven't been to any of our old card-parties either of late, have you? At least, I haven't seen you. I've gone to two or three, thinking you might be there."

That was another thing Arthur had done — broken up her interest in these old store and neighborhood parties and a banjo-and-mandolin club to which she had once belonged. They had all seemed so pleasing and amusing in the old days — but now — * * * * In those days Bart had been her usual companion when his work permitted.

"No," she replied evasively, but with a forced air of pleasant re-
membrance; "I have often thought of how much fun we had at those,
though. It was a shame to drop them. You haven't seen Harry Stull or
Trina Task recently, have you?" she inquired, more to be saying something than for any interest she felt.

He shook his head negatively, then added:

"Yes, I did, too; here in the waiting-room a few nights ago. They were
coming down-town to a theater, I suppose."

His face fell slightly as he recalled how it had been their custom to do
this, and what their one quarrel had been about. Shirley noticed it. She
felt the least bit sorry for him, but much more for herself, coming back
so disconsolately to all this.

"Well, you're looking as pretty as ever, Shirley," he continued, noting
that she had not written the telegram and that there was something
wistful in her glance. "Prettier, I think," and she smiled sadly. Every
word that she tolerated from him was as so much gold to him, so much
of dead ashes to her. "You wouldn't like to come down some evening this
week and see 'The Mouse-Trap,' would you? We haven't been to a
theater together in I don't know when." His eyes sought hers in a
hopeful, doglike way.

So — she could have him again — that was the pity of it! To have what
she really did not want, did not care for! At the least nod now he would
come, and this very devotion made it all but worthless, and so sad. She
ought to marry him now for certain, if she began in this way, and could
in a month's time if she chose, but oh, oh — could she? For the moment
she decided that she could not, would not. If he had only repulsed her —
told her to go — ignored her — but no; it was her fate to be loved by him
in this moving, pleading way, and hers not to love him as she wished to
love — to be loved. Plainly, he needed some one like her, whereas she,
she ——. She turned a little sick, a sense of the sacrilege of gaiety at this
time creeping into her voice, and exclaimed:

"No, no!" Then seeing his face change, a heavy sadness come over it,
"Not this week, anyhow, I mean" ("Not so soon," she had almost said). "I
have several engagements this week and I'm not feeling well. But" —
seeing his face change, and the thought of her own state returning —
"you might come out to the house some evening instead, and then we
can go some other time."

His face brightened intensely. It was wonderful how he longed to be
with her, how the least favor from her comforted and lifted him up. She
could see also now, however, how little it meant to her, how little it
could ever mean, even if to him it was heaven. The old relationship
would have to be resumed in toto, once and for all, but did she want it

that way now that she was feeling so miserable about this other affair? As she meditated, these various moods racing to and fro in her mind, Barton seemed to notice, and now it occurred to him that perhaps he had not pursued her enough — was too easily put off. She probably did like him yet. This evening, her present visit, seemed to prove it.

"Sure, sure!" he agreed. "I'd like that. I'll come out Sunday, if you say. We can go any time to the play. I'm sorry, Shirley, if you're not feeling well. I've thought of you a lot these days. I'll come out Wednesday, if you don't mind."

She smiled a wan smile. It was all so much easier than she had expected — her triumph — and so ashenlike in consequence, a flavor of dead-sea fruit and defeat about it all, that it was pathetic. How could she, after Arthur? How could he, really?

"Make it Sunday," she pleaded, naming the farthest day off, and then hurried out.

Her faithful lover gazed after her, while she suffered an intense nausea. To think — to think — it should all be coming to this! She had not used her telegraph-blank, and now had forgotten all about it. It was not the simple trickery that discouraged her, but her own future which could find no better outlet than this, could not rise above it apparently, or that she had no heart to make it rise above it. Why couldn't she interest herself in some one different to Barton? Why did she have to return to him? Why not wait and meet some other — ignore him as before? But no, no; nothing mattered now — no one — it might as well be Barton really as any one, and she would at least make him happy and at the same time solve her own problem. She went out into the train-shed and climbed into her train. Slowly, after the usual pushing and jostling of a crowd, it drew out toward Latonia, that suburban region in which her home lay. As she rode, she thought.

"What have I just done? What am I doing?" she kept asking herself as the clacking wheels on the rails fell into a rhythmic dance and the houses of the brown, dry, endless city fled past in a maze. "Severing myself decisively from the past — the happy past — for supposing, once I am married, Arthur should return and want me again — suppose! Suppose!"

Below at one place, under a shed, were some market-gardeners disposing of the last remnants of their day's wares — a sickly, dull life, she thought. Here was Rutgers Avenue, with its line of red street-cars, many wagons and tracks and counter-streams of automobiles — how often had she passed it morning and evening in a shuttle-like way, and how often would, unless she got married! And here, now, was the river flowing smoothly between its banks lined with coal-pockets and wharves — away,

away to the huge deep sea which she and Arthur had enjoyed so much. Oh, to be in a small boat and drift out, out into the endless, restless, pathless deep! Somehow the sight of this water, to-night and every night, brought back those evenings in the open with Arthur at Sparrows Point, the long line of dancers in Eckert's Pavilion, the woods at Atholby, the park, with the dancers in the pavilion — she choked back a sob. Once Arthur had come this way with her on just such an evening as this, pressing her hand and saying how wonderful she was. Oh, Arthur! Arthur! And now Barton was to take his old place again — forever, no doubt. She could not trifle with her life longer in this foolish way, or his. What was the use? But think of it!

Yes, it must be — forever now, she told herself. She must marry. Time would be slipping by and she would become too old. It was her only future — marriage. It was the only future she had ever contemplated really, a home, children, the love of some man whom she could love as she loved Arthur. Ah, what a happy home that would have been for her! But now, now——

But there must be no turning back now, either. There was no other way. If Arthur ever came back — but fear not, he wouldn't! She had risked so much and lost — lost him. Her little venture into true love had been such a failure. Before Arthur had come all had been well enough. Barton, stout and simple and frank and direct, had in some way — how, she could scarcely realize now — offered sufficient of a future. But now, now! He had enough money, she knew, to build a cottage for the two of them. He had told her so. He would do his best always to make her happy, she was sure of that. They could live in about the state her parents were living in — or a little better, not much — and would never want. No doubt there would be children, because he craved them — several of them — and that would take up her time, long years of it — the sad, gray years! But then Arthur, whose children she would have thrilled to bear, would be no more, a mere memory — think of that! — and Barton, the dull, the commonplace, would have achieved his finest dream — and why?

Because love was a failure for her — that was why — and in her life there could be no more true love. She would never love any one again as she had Arthur. It could not be, she was sure of it. He was too fascinating, too wonderful. Always, always, wherever she might be, whoever she might marry, he would be coming back, intruding between her and any possible love, receiving any possible kiss. It would be Arthur she would be loving or kissing. She dabbed at her eyes with a tiny handkerchief, turned her face close to the window and stared out, and then as the environs of Latonia came into view, wondered (so deep is romance):

What if Arthur should come back at some time — or now! Supposing he should be here at the station now, accidentally or on purpose, to welcome her, to soothe her weary heart. He had met her here before. How she would fly to him, lay her head on his shoulder, forget forever that Barton ever was, that they had ever separated for an hour. Oh, Arthur! Arthur!

But no, no; here was Latonia — here the viaduct over her train, the long business street and the cars marked "Center" and "Langdon Avenue" running back into the great city. A few blocks away in tree-shaded Bethune Street, duller and plainer than ever, was her parents' cottage and the routine of that old life which was now, she felt, more fully fastened upon her than ever before — the lawn-mowers, the lawns, the front porches all alike. Now would come the going to and fro of Barton to business as her father and she now went to business, her keeping house, cooking, washing, ironing, sewing for Barton as her mother now did these things for her father and herself. And she would not be in love really, as she wanted to be. Oh, dreadful! She could never escape it really, now that she could endure it less, scarcely for another hour. And yet she must, must, for the sake of — for the sake of — she closed her eyes and dreamed.

She walked up the street under the trees, past the houses and lawns all alike to her own, and found her father on their veranda reading the evening paper. She sighed at the sight.

"Back, daughter?" he called pleasantly.

"Yes."

"Your mother is wondering if you would like steak or liver for dinner. Better tell her."

"Oh, it doesn't matter."

She hurried into her bedroom, threw down her hat and gloves, and herself on the bed to rest silently, and groaned in her soul. To think that it had all come to this! — Never to see him any more! — To see only Barton, and marry him and live in such a street, have four or five children, forget all her youthful companionships — and all to save her face before her parents, and her future. Why must it be? Should it be, really? She choked and stifled. After a little time her mother, hearing her come in, came to the door — thin, practical, affectionate, conventional.

"What's wrong, honey? Aren't you feeling well to-night? Have you a headache? Let me feel."

Her thin cool fingers crept over her temples and hair. She suggested something to eat or a headache powder right away.

"I'm all right, mother. I'm just not feeling well now. Don't bother. I'll get up soon. Please don't."

"Would you rather have liver or steak to-night, dear?"

"Oh, anything—nothing—please don't bother—steak will do—anything"—if only she could get rid of her and be at rest!

. Her mother looked at her and shook her head sympathetically, then retreated quietly, saying no more. Lying so, she thought and thought—grinding, destroying thoughts about the beauty of the past, the darkness of the future—until able to endure them no longer she got up and, looking distractedly out of the window into the yard and the house next door, stared at her future fixedly. What should she do? What should she really do? There was Mrs. Kessel in her kitchen getting her dinner as usual, just as her own mother was now, and Mr. Kessel out on the front porch in his shirt-sleeves reading the evening paper. Beyond was Mr. Pollard in his yard, cutting the grass. All along Bethune Street were such houses and such people—simple, commonplace souls all—clerks, managers, fairly successful craftsmen, like her father and Barton, excellent in their way but not like Arthur the beloved, the lost—and here was she, perforce, or by decision of necessity, soon to be one of them, in some such street as this no doubt, forever and—. For the moment it choked and stifled her.

She decided that she would not. No, no, no! There must be some other way—many ways. She did not have to do this unless she really wished to—would not—only—. Then going to the mirror she looked at her face and smoothed her hair.

"But what's the use?" she asked of herself wearily and resignedly after a time. "Why should I cry? Why shouldn't I marry Barton? I don't amount to anything, anyhow. Arthur wouldn't have me. I wanted him, and I am compelled to take some one else—or no one—what difference does it really make who? My dreams are too high, that's all. I wanted Arthur, and he wouldn't have me. I don't want Barton, and he crawls at my feet. I'm a failure, that's what's the matter with me."

And then, turning up her sleeves and removing a fichu which stood out too prominently from her breast, she went into the kitchen and, looking about for an apron, observed:

"Can't I help? Where's the tablecloth?" and finding it among napkins and silverware in a drawer in the adjoining room, proceeded to set the table.

Married[1]

IN CONNECTION with their social adjustment, one to the other, during the few months they had been together, there had occurred a number of things which made clearer to Duer and Marjorie the problematic relationship which existed between them, though it must be confessed it was clearer chiefly to him. The one thing which had been troubling Duer was not whether he would fit agreeably into her social dreams — he knew he would, so great was her love for him — but whether she would fit herself into his. Of all his former friends, he could think of only a few who would be interested in Marjorie, or she in them. She cared nothing for the studio life, except as it concerned him, and he knew no other.

Because of his volatile, enthusiastic temperament, it was easy to see, now that she was with him constantly, that he could easily be led into one relationship and another which concerned her not at all. He was for running here, there, and everywhere, just as he had before marriage, and it was very hard for him to see that Marjorie should always be with him. As a matter of fact, it occurred to him as strange that she should want to be. She would not be interested in all the people he knew, he thought. Now that he was living with her and observing her more closely, he was quite sure that most of the people he had known in the past, even in an indifferent way, would not appeal to her at all.

Take Cassandra Draper, for instance, or Neva Badger, or Edna Bainbridge, with her budding theatrical talent, or Cornelia Skiff, or Volida Blackstone — any of these women of the musical art-studio world with their radical ideas, their indifference to appearances, their semisecret immorality. And yet any of these women would be glad to see him socially, unaccompanied by his wife, and he would be glad to see them. He liked them. Most of them had not seen Marjorie, but, if they had, he fancied that they would feel about her much as he did — that is, that she

---

1. "Married" first appeared in *Cosmopolitan*, September 1917.

did not like them, really did not fit with their world. She could not understand their point of view, he saw that. She was for one life, one love. All this excitement about entertainment, their gathering in this studio and that, this meeting of radicals and models and budding theatrical stars which she had heard him and others talking about — she suspected of it no good results. It was too feverish, too far removed from the commonplace of living to which she had been accustomed. She had been raised on a farm where, if she was not actually a farmer's daughter, she had witnessed what a real struggle for existence meant.

Out in Iowa, in the neighborhood of Avondale, there were no artists, no models, no budding actresses, no incipient playwrights, such as Marjorie found here about her. There, people worked, and worked hard. Her father was engaged at this minute in breaking the soil of his fields for the spring planting — an old man with a white beard, an honest, kindly eye, a broad, kindly charity, a sense of duty. Her mother was bending daily over a cook-stove, preparing meals, washing dishes, sewing clothes, mending socks, doing the thousand and one chores which fall to the lot of every good housewife and mother. Her sister Cecily, for all her gaiety and beauty, was helping her mother, teaching school, going to church, and taking the commonplace facts of mid-Western life in a simple, good-natured, unambitious way. And there was none of that toplofty sense of superiority which marked the manner of these Eastern upstarts.

Duer had suggested that they give a tea, and decided that they should invite Charlotte Russell and Mildred Ayres, who were both still conventionally moral in their liberalism; Francis Hatton, a young sculptor, and Miss Ollie Stearns, the latter because she had a charming contralto voice and could help them entertain. Marjorie was willing to invite both Miss Russell and Miss Ayres, not because she really wanted to know either of them but because she did not wish to appear arbitrary and especially contrary. In her estimation, Duer liked these people too much. They were friends of too long standing. She reluctantly wrote them to come, and because they liked Duer and because they wished to see the kind of wife he had, they came.

There was no real friendship to be established between Marjorie and Miss Ayres, however, for their outlook on life was radically different, though Miss Ayres was as conservative as Marjorie in her attitude, and as set in her convictions. But the latter had decided, partly because Duer had neglected her, partly because Marjorie was the victor in this contest, that he had made a mistake; she was convinced that Marjorie had not sufficient artistic apprehension, sufficient breadth of outlook, to make a good wife for him. She was charming enough to look at, of course, she had discovered that in her first visit; but there was really not enough in her socially, she was not sufficiently trained in the ways of the world, not sufficiently wise and interesting to make him an ideal companion. In addition she insisted on thinking this vigorously and, smile as she might and be as gracious as she might, it showed in her manner. Marjorie noticed it. Duer did, too. He did not dare intimate to either what he thought, but he felt that there would be no peace. It worried him, for he liked Mildred very much; but, alas! Marjorie had no good to say of her.

As for Charlotte Russell, he was grateful to her for the pleasant manner in which she steered between Scylla and Charybdis. She saw at once what Marjorie's trouble was, and did her best to allay suspicions by treating Duer formally in her presence. It was "Mr. Wilde" here and "Mr. Wilde" there, with most of her remarks addressed to Marjorie; but she did not find it easy sailing, after all. Marjorie was suspicious. There was none of the old freedom any more which had existed between Charlotte and Duer. He saw, by Marjorie's manner, the moment he became the least exuberant and free that it would not do. That evening he said, forgetting himself:

"Hey, Charlotte, you skate! Come over here. I want to show you something."

He forgot all about it afterward, but Marjorie reminded him.

"Honey," she began, when she was in his arms before the fire, and he was least expecting it, "what makes you be so free with people when they call here? You're not the kind of man that can really afford to be free with any one. Don't you know you can't? You're too big; you're too great. You just belittle yourself when you do it, and it makes them think that they are your equal when they are not."

"Who has been acting free now?" he asked sourly, on the instant, and yet with a certain make-believe of manner, dreading the storm of feeling, the atmosphere of censure and control which this remark forboded.

"Why, you have!" she persisted correctively, and yet apparently mildly and innocently. "You always do. You don't exercise enough dignity, dearie. It isn't that you haven't it naturally — you just don't exercise it. I know how it is; you forget."

Duer stirred with opposition at this, for she was striking him on his tenderest spot — his pride. It was true that he did lack dignity at times. He knew it. Because of his affection for the beautiful or interesting things — women, men, dramatic situations, songs, anything — he sometimes became very gay and free, talking loudly, using slang expressions, laughing boisterously. It was a failing with him, he knew. He carried it to excess at times. His friends, his most intimate ones in the musical profession had noted it before this. In his own heart he regretted these things afterward, but he couldn't help them, apparently. He liked excitement, freedom, gaiety — naturalness, as he called it — it helped him in his musical work, but it hurt him tremendously if he thought that any one else noticed it as out of the ordinary. He was exceedingly sensitive, and this developing line of criticism of Marjorie's was something new to him. He had never noticed anything of that in her before marriage.

Up to the time of the ceremony, and for a little while afterward, it had appeared to him as if he were lord and master. She had always seemed so dependent on him, so anxious that he should take her. Why, her very life had been in his hands, as it were, or so he had thought! And now — he tried to think back over the evening and see what it was he had done or said, but he couldn't remember anything. Everything seemed innocent enough. He couldn't recall a single thing, and yet——

"I don't know what you're talking about," he replied sourly, withdrawing into himself. "I haven't noticed that I lack dignity so much. I have a right to be cheerful, haven't I? You seem to be finding a lot that's wrong with me."

"Now please don't get angry, Duer," she persisted, anxious to apply the corrective measure of her criticism, but willing, at the same time, to use the quickness of his sympathy for her obvious weakness and apparent helplessness to shield herself from him. "I can't ever tell you anything if you're going to be angry. You don't lack dignity generally, honeybun! You only forget at times. Don't you know how it is?"

She was cuddling up to him, her voice quavering, her hand stroking his cheek, in a curious effort to combine affection and punishment at the same time. Duer felt nothing but wrath, resentment, discouragement, failure.

"No, I don't," he replied crossly. "What did I do? I don't recall doing anything that was so very much out of the way."

"It wasn't that it was so very much, honey; it was just the way you did it. You forget, I know. But it doesn't look right. It belittles you."

"What did I do?" he insisted impatiently.

"Why, it wasn't anything so very much. It was just when you had the pictures of those new sculptures which Mr. Hatton lent you, and you were showing them to Miss Russell. Don't you remember what you said — how you called her over to you?"

"No," he answered, having by now completely forgotten. He was thinking that accidentally he might have slipped his arm about Charlotte, or that he might have said something out of the way jestingly about the pictures; but Marjorie could not have heard. He was so careful these days, anyway.

"Why, you said: 'Hey, Charlotte, you skate! Come over here.' Now, what a thing to say to a girl! Don't you see how ugly it sounds, how vulgar? She can't enjoy that sort of remark, particularly in my presence, do you think? She must know that I can't like it, that I'd rather you wouldn't talk that way, particularly here. And if she were the right sort of girl she wouldn't want you to talk to her at all that way. Don't you know she wouldn't? She couldn't. Now, really, no good woman would, would she?"

Duer flushed angrily. Good heaven! Were such innocent, simple things as this to be made the subject of comment and criticism! Was his life, because of his sudden, infatuated marriage, to be pulled down to a level he had never previously even contemplated? Why — why — This catechising, so new to his life, so different to anything he had ever endured in his youth or since, was certain to irritate him greatly, to be a constant thorn in his flesh. It cut him to the core. He got up, putting Marjorie away from him, for they were sitting in a big chair before the fire, and walked to the window.

"I don't see that at all," he said stubbornly. "I don't see anything in that remark to raise a row about. Why, for goodness' sake! I have known Charlotte Russell — for years and years, it seems, although it has only been a little while at that. She's like a sister to me. I like her. She doesn't mind what I say. I'd stake my life she never thought anything about it. No one would who likes me as well as she does. Why do you pitch on that to make a fuss about, for heaven's sake?"

"Please don't swear, Duer," exclaimed Marjorie anxiously, using this expression for criticising him further. "It isn't nice in you, and it doesn't sound right toward me. I'm your wife. It doesn't make any difference how long you've known her; I don't think it's nice to talk to her in that way, particularly in my presence. You say you've known her so well and you like her so much. Very well. But don't you think you ought to consider me a little, now that I'm your wife? Don't you think that you oughtn't to want to do anything like that any more, even if you have known her so well — don't you think? You're married now, and it doesn't look right to others, whatever you think of me. It can't look right to her, if she's as nice as you say she is."

Duer listened to this semipleading, semichastising harangue with disturbed, opposed, and irritated ears. Certainly, there was some truth in what she said; but wasn't it an awfully small thing to raise a row about? Why should she quarrel with him for that? Couldn't he ever be lightsome in his form of address any more? It was true that it did sound a little rough, now that he thought of it. Perhaps it wasn't exactly the thing to say in her presence, but Charlotte didn't mind. They had known each other much too long. She hadn't noticed it one way or the other; and here was

Marjorie charging him with being vulgar and inconsiderate, and Charlotte with being not the right sort of girl, and practically vulgar, also, on account of it. It was too much. It was too narrow, too conventional. He wasn't going to tolerate anything like that permanently.

He was about to say something mean in reply, make some cutting commentary, when Marjorie came over to him. She saw that she had lashed him and Charlotte and his generally easy attitude pretty thoroughly, and that he was becoming angry. Perhaps, because of his sensitiveness, he would avoid this sort of thing in the future. Anyhow, now that she had lived with him four months, she was beginning to understand him better, to see the quality of his moods, the strength of his passions, the nature of his weaknesses, how quickly he responded to the blandishments of pretended sorrow, joy, affection, or distress. She thought she could reform him at her leisure. She saw that he looked upon her in his superior way as a little girl — largely because of the size of her body. He seemed to think that, because she was little, she must be weak, whereas she knew that she had the use and the advantage of a wisdom, a tactfulness and a subtlety of which he did not even dream. Compared to her he was not nearly as wise as he thought, at least in matters relating to the affections. Hence, any appeal to his sympathies, his strength, almost invariably produced a reaction from any antagonistic mood in which she might have placed him. She saw him now as a mother might see a great, overgrown, sulking boy, needing only to be coaxed to be brought out of a very unsatisfactory condition, and she decided to bring him out of it. For a short period in her life she had taught children in school, and knew the incipient moods of the race very well.

"Now, Duer," she coaxed, "you're not really going to be angry with me, are you? You're not going to be 'mad to me'?" (imitating childish language).

"Oh, don't bother, Marjorie," he replied distantly. "It's all right. No; I'm not angry. Only let's not talk about it any more."

"You are angry, though, Duer," she wheedled, slipping her arm around him. "Please don't be mad to me. I'm sorry now. I talk too much. I get mad. I know I oughtn't. Please don't be mad at me, honey-bun. I'll get over this after a while. I'll do better. Please, I will. Please don't be mad, will you?"

He could not stand this coaxing very long. Just as he thought, he did look upon her as a child, and this pathetic baby-talk was irresistible. He smiled grimly after a while. She was so little. He ought to endure her idiosyncrasies of temperament. Besides, he had never treated her right. He had not been faithful to his engagement-vows. If she only knew how bad he really was!

Marjorie slipped her arm through his and stood leaning against him. She loved this tall, slender, distinguished-looking youth, and she wanted to take care of him. She thought that she was doing this now, when she called attention to his faults. Some day, by her persistent efforts maybe, he would overcome these silly, disagreeable, offensive traits. He would overcome being undignified; he would see that he needed to show her more consideration than he now seemed to think he did. He would learn that he was married. He would become a quiet, reserved, forceful man, weary of the silly women who were buzzing round him solely because he was a musician and talented and good-looking, and then he would be truly great. She knew what they wanted, these nasty women — they would like to have him for themselves. Well, they wouldn't get him. And they needn't think they would. She had him. He had married her. And she was going to keep him. They could just buzz all they pleased, but they wouldn't get him. So there!

There had been other spats following this — one relating to Duer not having told his friends of his marriage for some little time afterward, an oversight which in his easy going bohemian brain augured no deep planted seed of disloyalty, but just a careless, indifferent way of doing things, whereas in hers it flowered as one of the most unpardonable things imaginable! Imagine any one in the Middle West doing anything like that — any one with a sound, sane conception of the responsibilities and duties of marriage, its inviolable character! For Marjorie, having come to this estate by means of a hardly won victory, was anxious lest any germ of inattentiveness, lack of consideration, alien interest, or affection flourish and become a raging disease which would imperil or destroy the conditions on which her happiness was based. After every encounter with Miss Ayres, for instance, whom she suspected of being one of his former flames, a girl who might have become his wife, there were fresh charges to be made. She didn't invite Marjorie to sit down sufficiently quickly when she called at her studio, was one complaint; she didn't offer her a cup of tea at the hour she called another afternoon, though it was quite time for it. She didn't invite her to sing or play on another occasion, though there were others there who were invited.

"I gave her one good shot, though," said Marjorie, one day, to Duer, in narrating her troubles. "She's always talking about her artistic friends. I as good as asked her why she didn't marry, if she is so much sought after."

Duer did not understand the mental sword-thrusts involved in these feminine bickerings. He was likely to be deceived by the airy geniality which sometimes accompanied the bitterest feeling. He could stand by listening to a conversation between Marjorie and Miss Ayres, or

Marjorie and any one else whom she did not like, and miss all the subtle stabs and cutting insinuations which were exchanged, and of which Marjorie was so thoroughly capable. He did not blame her for fighting for herself if she thought she was being injured, but he did object to her creating fresh occasions, and this, he saw, she was quite capable of doing. She was constantly looking for new opportunities to fight with Mildred Ayres and Miss Russell or any one else whom she thought he truly liked, whereas with those in whom he could not possibly be interested she was genial (and even affectionate) enough. But Duer also thought that Mildred might be better engaged than in creating fresh difficulties. Truly, he had thought better of her. It seemed a sad commentary on the nature of friendship between men and women, and he was sorry.

But, nevertheless, Marjorie found a few people whom she felt to be of her own kind. M. Bland, who had sponsored Duer's first piano recital a few months before, invited Duer and Marjorie to a — for them — quite sumptuous dinner at the Plaza, where they met Sydney Borg, the musical critic of an evening paper; Melville Ogden Morris, curator of the Museum of Fine Arts, and his wife; Joseph Newcorn, one of the wealthy sponsors of the opera and its geniuses, and Mrs. Newcorn. Neither Duer nor Marjorie had ever seen a private dining-room set in so scintillating a manner. It fairly glittered with Sèvres and Venetian tinted glass. The wine-goblets were seven in number, set in an ascending row. The order of food was complete from Russian caviare to dessert, black coffee, nuts, liqueurs, and cigars.

The conversation wandered its intense intellectual way from American musicians and singers, European painters and sculptors, discoveries of ancient pottery in the isles of the Ægean, to the manufacture of fine glass on Long Island, the character of certain collectors and collections of paintings in America, and the present state of the Fine Arts Museum. Duer listened eagerly, for, as yet, he was a little uncertain of himself his position in the art world. He did not quite know how to take these fine and able personages who seemed so powerful in the world's affairs. Joseph Newcorn, as M. Bland calmly indicated to him, must be worth in the neighborhood of fifteen million dollars. He thought nothing, so he said, of paying ten, fifteen, twenty, thirty thousand dollars for a picture if it appealed to him. Mr. Morris was a graduate of Harvard, formerly curator of a Western museum, the leader of one of the excavating expeditions to Melos in the Grecian Archipelago. Sydney Borg was a student of musical history, who appeared to have a wide knowledge of art tendencies here and abroad, but who, nevertheless, wrote musical criticisms for a living. He was a little man of Norse extraction on his father's side, but, as he laughingly admitted, born and raised in McKeesport, Pennsylvania. He liked Duer for his simple acknowledgment of the fact that he came from a small town in the Middle West, and a drug business out in Illinois.

"It's curious how our nation brings able men from the ranks," he said to Duer. "It's one of the great, joyous, hopeful facts about this country."

"Yes," said Duer; "that's why I like it so much."

Duer thought, as he dined here, how strange America was, with its mixture of races, its unexpected sources of talent, its tremendous wealth and confidence. His own beginning, so very humble at first, so very promising now — one of the most talked of pianists of his day — was in its way an illustration of its resources in so far as talent was concerned. Mr. Newcorn, who had once been a tailor, so he was told, and his wife was another case in point. They were such solid, unemotional, practical-looking people, and yet he could see that this solid looking man whom some musicians might possibly have sneered at for his self-complacency and curiously accented English, was as wise and sane and keen and kindly as any one present, perhaps more so, and as wise in matters musical. The only difference between him and the average American was that he was exceptionally practical and not given to nervous enthusiasm. Marjorie liked him, too.

It was at this particular dinner that the thought occurred to Marjorie that the real merit of the art and musical world was not so much in the noisy studio palaver which she heard at so many places frequented by Duer, in times past at least — Charlotte Russell's, Mildred Ayres's and elsewhere — but in the solid commercial achievements of such men as Joseph Newcorn, Georges Bland, Melville Ogden Morris, and Sydney Borg. She liked the laconic "Yes, yes," of Mr. Newcorn, when anything was said that suited him particularly well, and his "I haf seen dat bardicular berformance" with which he interrupted several times when Grand Opera and its stars were up for consideration. She was thinking if only a man like that would take an interest in Duer, how much better it would be for him than all the enthusiasm of these silly noisy studio personalities. She was glad to see also that, intellectually, Duer could hold his own with any and all of these people. He was as much at ease here with Mr. Morris, talking about Greek excavations, as he was with Mr. Borg, discussing American musical conditions. She could not make out much what it was all about, but, of course, it must be very important if these men discussed it. Duer was not sure as yet whether any one knew much more about life than he did. He suspected not, but it might be that some of these eminent curators, art critics, bankers, and managers like M. Bland, had a much wider insight into practical affairs. Practical affairs — he thought. If he only knew something about money! Somehow, though, his mind could not grasp how money was made. It seemed so easy for some people, but for him a grim, dark mystery.

After this dinner it was that Marjorie began to feel that Duer ought to be especially careful with whom he associated. She had talked with Mrs. Newcorn and Mrs. Morris, and found them simple, natural people like herself. They were not puffed up with vanity and self-esteem, as were those other men and women to whom Duer had thus far introduced her. As compared to Charlotte Russell and Mildred Ayres or her own mother and sisters and her Western friends, they were more like the latter. Mrs. Newcorn, wealthy as she was, spoke of her two sons and three daughters as any good-natured, solicitous mother would. One of her sons was at Harvard, the other at Yale. She asked Marjorie to come and see her some time, and gave her her address. Mrs. Morris was more cultured apparently, more given to books and art; but even she was interested in what, to Marjorie, were the more important or, at least, more necessary things, the things on which all art and culture primarily based themselves — the commonplace and necessary details of the home. Cooking, housekeeping, shopping, sewing, were not beneath her consideration, as indeed they were not below Mrs. Newcorn's. The former spoke of having to go and look for a new spring bonnet in the morning, and how difficult it was to find the time. Once when the men were getting especially excited about European and American artistic standards, Marjorie asked:

"Are you very much interested in art, Mrs. Morris?"

"Not so very much, to tell you the truth, Mrs. Wilde. Oh, I like some pictures, and I hear most of the important recitals each season, but, as I often tell my husband, when you have one baby two years old and another of five and another of seven, it takes considerable time to attend to the art of raising them. I let him do the art for the family, and I take care of the home."

This was sincere consolation for Marjorie. Up to this time she appeared to be in danger of being swamped by this artistic storm which she had encountered. Her arts of cooking, sewing, housekeeping, appeared as nothing in this vast palaver about music, painting, sculpture, books and the like. She knew nothing, as she had most painfully discovered recently, of Strauss, Dvořák, Debussy, almost as little of Cézanne, Gauguin, Matisse, Van Gogh, Rodin, Ibsen, Shaw and Maeterlinck, with whom the studios were apparently greatly concerned. And when people talked of singers, musicians, artists, sculptors, and playwrights, often she was compelled to keep silent, whereas Duer could stand with his elbow on some mantel or piano and discuss by the half hour or hour individuals of whom she had never heard — Verlaine, Tchaikowsky, Tolstoy, Turgenieff, Tagore, Dostoyevsky, Whistler, Velasquez — anybody and everybody who appeared to interest the studio element. It was positively frightening.

A phase of this truth was that because of his desire to talk, his pleasure in meeting people, his joy in hearing of new things, his sense of the dramatic, Duer could catch quickly and retain vigorously anything which related to social, artistic, or intellectual development. He had no idea of what a full-orbed, radiant, receptive thing his mind was. He only knew that life, things, intellect — anything and everything — gave him joy when he was privileged to look into them, whereas Marjorie was not so keenly minded artistically, and he gave as freely as he received. In this whirl of discussion, this lofty transcendentalism, Marjorie was all but lost; but she clung tenaciously to the hope that, somehow, affection, regard for the material needs of her husband, the care of his clothes, the preparation of his meals, the serving of him quite as would a faithful slave, would bind him to her. At once and quickly, she hated and feared these artistically arrayed, artistically minded, vampirish-looking maidens and women who appeared from this quarter and that to talk to Duer, all of whom apparently had known him quite well in the past — since he had come to New York. When she would see him standing or leaning somewhere, intent on the rendering of a song, the narration of some dramatic incident, the description of some book or picture, or personage, by this or that delicately chiseled Lorelei of the art or music or dramatic world, her heart contracted ominously and a nameless dread seized her. Somehow, these creatures, however intent they might be on their work, or however indifferent actually to the artistic charms of her husband, seemed to be intent on taking him from her. She saw how easily and naturally he smiled, how very much at home he seemed to be in their company, how surely he gravitated to the type of girl who was beautifully and artistically dressed, who had ravishing eyes, fascinating hair, a sylphlike figure, and vivacity of manner — or how naturally they gravitated to him. In the rush of conversation and the exchange of greetings he was apt to forget her, to stroll about by himself engaging in conversation first with one and then another, while she stood or sat somewhere gazing nervously or regretfully on, unable to hold her own in the cross-fire of conversation, unable to retain the interest of most of the selfish, lovesick, sensation-seeking girls and men.

They always began talking about the opera, or the play, or the latest sensation in society, or some new singer or dancer or poet, and Marjorie, being new to this atmosphere and knowing so little of it, was compelled to confess that she did not know. It chagrined, dazed, and frightened her for a time. She longed to be able to grasp quickly and learn what this was all about. She wondered where she had been living — how — to have missed all this. Why, goodness gracious, these things were enough to wreck her married life! Duer would think so poorly of her — how could he help it? She watched these girls and women talking to him, and by turns, while imitating them as best she could, became envious, fearful, regretful, angry; charging, first, herself with unfitness; next, Duer with neglect; next, these people with insincerity, immorality, vanity; and lastly, the whole world and life with a conspiracy to cheat her out of what was rightfully her own. Why wouldn't these people be nice to her? Why didn't they give of their time and patience to make her comfortable and at home — as freely, say, as they did to him? Wasn't she his wife, now? Why did Duer neglect her? Why did they hang on his words in their eager, seductive, alluring way? She hated them and, at moments, she hated him, only to be struck by a terrifying wave of remorse and fear a moment later. What if he should grow tired of her? What if his love should change? He had seemed so enamored of her only a little while before they were married, so taken by what he called her naturalness, grace, simplicity and emotional pull.

On one of these occasions, or rather after it, when they had returned from an evening at Francis Hatton's at which she felt that she had been neglected, she threw herself disconsolately into Duer's arms and exclaimed:

"What's the matter with me, Duer? Why am I so dull — so uninteresting — so worthless?"

The sound of her voice was pathetic, helpless, vibrant with the quality of an unuttered sob, a quality which had appealed to him intensely long before they were married, and now he stirred nervously.

"Why, what's the matter with you now, Margie?" he asked sympathetically, sure that a new storm of some sort was coming. "What's come over you? There's nothing the matter with you. Why do you ask? Who's been saying there is?"

"Oh, nothing, nothing — nobody! Everybody! Everything!" exclaimed Marjorie dramatically, and bursting into tears. "I see how it is. I see what is the matter with me. Oh! Oh! It's because I don't know anything, I suppose. It's because I'm not fit to associate with you. It's because I haven't had the training that some people have had. It's because I'm dull! Oh! Oh!" and a torrent of heart-breaking sobs which shook her frame from head to toe followed the outburst and declamation.

Duer, always moved by her innate emotional force and charm, whatever other lack he had reason to bewail, gazed before him in startled sympathy, astonishment, pain, wonder, for he was seeing very clearly and keenly in these echoing sounds what the trouble was. She was feeling neglected, outclassed, unconsidered, helpless; and because it was more or less true it was frightening and wounding her. She was, for the first time no doubt, beginning to feel the tragedy of life, its uncertainty, its pathos and injury, as he so often had. Hitherto her home, her relatives and friends had more or less protected her from that, for she had come from a happy home, but now she was out and away from all that and had only him. Of course she had been neglected. He remembered that now. It was partly his fault, partly the fault of surrounding conditions. But what could he do about it? What say? People had conditions fixed for them in this world by their own ability. Perhaps he should not have married her at all, but how should he comfort her in this crisis? How say something that would ease her soul?

"Why, Margie," he said seriously, "you know that's not true! You know you're not dull. Your manners and your taste and your style are as good as those of anybody. Who has hinted that they aren't? What has come over you? Who has been saying anything to you? Have I done anything? If so, I'm sorry!" He had a guilty consciousness of misrepresenting himself and his point of view even while saying this, but kindness, generosity, affection, her legal right to his affection, as he now thought, demanded it.

"No! No!" she exclaimed brokenly and without ceasing her tears. "It isn't you. It isn't anybody. It's me — just me! That's what's the matter with me. I'm dull; I'm not stylish; I'm not attractive. I don't know anything about music or books or people or anything. I sit and listen, but I don't know what to say. People talk to you — they hang on your words — but they haven't anything to say to me. They can't talk to me, and I can't talk to them. It's because I don't know anything — because I haven't anything to say! Oh dear! Oh dear!" and she beat her thin, artistic little hands on the shoulders of his coat.

Duer could not endure this storm without an upwelling of pity for her. He cuddled her close in his arms, extremely sad that she should be compelled to suffer so. What should he do? What could he do? He could see how it was. She was hurt; she was neglected. He neglected her when among others. These smart women whom he knew and liked to talk with neglected her. They couldn't see in her what he could. Wasn't life pathetic? They didn't know how sweet she was, how faithful, how glad she was to work for him. That really didn't make any difference in the art world, he knew, but still it almost seemed as if it ought to. There one must be clever, he knew that — everybody knew it. And Marjorie was not clever — at least, not in their way. She couldn't play or sing or paint or talk brilliantly, as they could. She did not really know what the world of music, art, and literature was doing. She was only good, faithful, excellent as a housewife, a fine mender of clothes, a careful buyer, saving, considerate, dependable, but——

As he thought of this and then of this upwelling depth of emotion of hers, a thing quite moving to him always, he realized, or thought he did, that no woman that he had ever known had anything quite like this. He had known many women intimately. He had associated with Charlotte and Mildred and Neva Badger and Volida Blackstone, and quite a number of interesting, attractive young women whom he had met here and there since, but outside of the stage—that art of Sarah Bernhardt and Clara Morris and some of the more talented English actresses of these later days—he persuaded himself that he had never seen any one quite like Marjorie. This powerful upwelling of emotion which she was now exhibiting and which was so distinctive of her, was not to be found elsewhere, he thought. He had felt it keenly the first days he had visited her at her father's home in Avondale. Oh, those days with her in Avondale! How wonderful they were! Those delicious nights! Flowers, moonlight, odors, came back—the green fields, the open sky. Yes; she was powerful emotionally. She was compounded of many and all of these things.

It was true she knew nothing of art, nothing of music—the great, new music—nothing of books in the eclectic sense, but she had real, sweet, deep, sad, stirring emotion, the most appealing thing he knew. It might not be as great as that exhibited by some of the masters of the stage, or the great composers—he was not quite sure, so critical is life—but nevertheless it was effective, dramatic, powerful. Where did she get it? No really common soul could have it. Here must be something of the loneliness of the prairies, the sad patience of the rocks and fields, the lonesomeness of the hush of the countryside at night, the aimless, monotonous, pathetic chirping of the crickets. Her father following down a furrow in the twilight behind straining, toil-worn horses; her brothers binding wheat in the July sun; the sadness of furrow scents and field fragrances in the twilight—there was something of all these things in her sobs.

It appealed to him, as it might well have to any artist. In his way Duer understood this, felt it keenly.

"Why, Margie," he insisted, "you mustn't talk like that! You're better than you say you are. You say you don't know anything about books or art or music. Why, that isn't all. There are things, many things, which are deeper than those things. Emotion is a great thing in itself, dearest, if you only knew. You have that. Sarah Bernhardt had it; Clara Morris had it, but who else? In 'La Dame aux Camelias,' 'Sapho,' 'Carmen,' 'Mademoiselle de Maupin,' it is written about, but it is never commonplace. It's great. I'd rather have your deep upwelling of emotion than all those cheap pictures, songs, and talk put together. For, sweet, don't you know" — and he cuddled her more closely — "great art is based on great emotion. There is really no great art without it. I know that best of all, being a musician. You may not have the power to express yourself in music or books or pictures — you play charmingly enough for me — but you have the thing on which these things are based; you have the power to feel them. Don't worry over yourself, dear. I see that, and I know what you are, whether any one else does or not. Don't worry over me. I have to be nice to these people. I like them in their way, but I love you. I married you — isn't that proof enough? What more do you want? Don't you understand, little Margie? Don't you see? Now aren't you going to cheer up and be happy? You have me. Ain't I enough, sweetie? Can't you be happy with just me? What more do you want? Just tell me."

"Nothing more, honey-bun!" she went on sobbing and cuddling close; "nothing more, if I can have you. Just you! That's all I want — you, you, you!"

She hugged him tight. Duer sighed secretly. He really did not believe all he said, but what of it? What else could he do, say, he asked himself? He was married to her. In his way, he loved her — or at least sympathized with her intensely.

"And am I emotionally great?" she cuddled and cooed, after she had held him tight for a few moments. "Doesn't it make any difference whether I know anything much about music or books or art? I do know something, don't I, honey? I'm not wholly ignorant, am I?"

"No, no, sweetie; how you talk!"

"And will you always love me whether I know anything or not, honey-bun?" she went on. "And won't it make any difference whether I can just cook and sew and do the marketing and keep house for you? And will you like me because I'm just pretty and not smart? I am a little pretty, ain't I, dear?"

"You're lovely," whispered Duer soothingly. "You're beautiful. Listen to me, sweet. I want to tell you something. Stop crying now, and dry your eyes, and I'll tell you something nice. Do you remember how we stood, one night, at the end of your father's field there near the barn-gate and saw him coming down the path, singing to himself, driving that team of big gray horses, his big straw hat on the back of his head and his sleeves rolled up above his elbows?"

"Yes," said Marjorie.

"Do you remember how the air smelled of roses and honeysuckle and cut hay — and oh, all those lovely scents of evening that we have out there in the country?"

"Yes," replied Marjorie interestedly.

"And do you remember how lovely I said the cow-bells sounded tinkling in the pasture where the little river ran?"

"Yes."

"And the fireflies beginning to flash in the trees?"

"Yes."

"And that sad, deep red in the West, where the sun had gone down?"

"Yes, I remember," said Marjorie, crushing her cheek to his neck.

"Now listen to me, honey: That water running over the bright stones in that little river; the grass spreading out, soft and green, over the slope; the cow-bells tinkling; the smoke curling up from your mother's chimney; your father looking like a patriarch out of Bible days coming home — all the soft sounds, all the sweet odors, all the carolling of birds — where do you suppose all that is now?"

"I don't know," replied Marjorie, anticipating something complimentary.

"It's here," he replied easily, drawing her close and petting her. "It's done up in one little body here in my arms. Your voice, your hair, your eyes, your pretty body, your emotional moods — where do you suppose they come from? Nature has a chemistry all her own. She's like a druggist sometimes, compounding things. She takes a little of the beauty of the sunset, of the sky, of the fields, of the water, of the flowers, of dreams and aspirations and simplicity and patience, and she makes a girl. And some parents somewhere have her, and then they name her 'Marjorie' and then they raise her nicely and innocently, and then a bold, bad man like Duer comes along and takes her, and then she cries because she thinks he doesn't see anything in her. Now, isn't that funny?"

"O-oh!" exclaimed Marjorie, melted by the fire of his feeling for beauty, the quaintness and sweetness of his diction, the subtlety of his compliment, the manner in which he coaxed her patiently out of herself.

"Oh, I love you, Duer dear! I love you, love you, love you! Oh, you're wonderful! You won't ever stop loving me, will you, dearest? You'll always be true to me, won't you, Duer? You'll never leave me, will you? I'll always be your little Margie, won't I? Oh, dear, I'm so happy!" and she hugged him closer and closer.

"No, no," and "Yes, yes," assured Duer, as the occasion demanded, as he stared patiently into the fire. This was not real passion to him, not real love in any sense, or at least he did not feel that it was. He was too

skeptical of himself, his life and love, however much he might sympathize with and be drawn to her. He was questioning himself at this very
time as to what it was that caused him to talk so. Was it sympathy, love of
beauty, power of poetic expression, delicacy of sentiment? — certainly
nothing more. Wasn't it this that was already causing him to be hailed as
a great musician? He believed so. Could he honestly say that he loved
Marjorie? No, he was sure that he couldn't, now that he had her and
realized her defects, as well as his own — his own principally. No; he
liked her, sympathized with her, felt sorry for her. That ability of his to
paint a picture in notes and musical phrases, to extract the last ringing
delicacy out of the keys of a piano, was at the bottom of this last
description. To Marjorie, for the moment, it might seem real enough,
but he — he was thinking of the truth of the picture she had painted of
herself. It was all so — every word she said. She was not really suited to
these people. She did not understand them; she never would. He would
always be soothing and coaxing, and she would always be crying and
worrying.

DOVER · THRIFT · EDITIONS

All books complete and unabridged. All 5³⁄₁₆″ × 8¼″, paperbound.
Just $1.00–$2.00 in U.S.A.

A selection of the more than 100 titles in the series:

FLATLAND: A ROMANCE OF MANY DIMENSIONS, Edwin A. Abbott. 96pp. 27263-X $1.00

DOVER BEACH AND OTHER POEMS, Matthew Arnold. 112pp. 28037-3 $1.00

CIVIL WAR STORIES, Ambrose Bierce. 128pp. 28038-1 $1.00

THE DEVIL'S DICTIONARY, Ambrose Bierce. 144pp. 27542-6 $1.00

SONGS OF INNOCENCE AND SONGS OF EXPERIENCE, William Blake. 64pp. 27051-3 $1.00

SONNETS FROM THE PORTUGUESE AND OTHER POEMS, Elizabeth Barrett Browning. 64pp. 27052-1 $1.00

MY LAST DUCHESS AND OTHER POEMS, Robert Browning. 128pp. 27783-6 $1.00

SELECTED POEMS, George Gordon, Lord Byron. 112pp. 27784-4 $1.00

ALICE'S ADVENTURES IN WONDERLAND, Lewis Carroll. 96pp. 27543-4 $1.00

O PIONEERS!, Willa Cather. 128pp. 27785-2 $1.00

THE CHERRY ORCHARD, Anton Chekhov. 64pp. 26682-6 $1.00

THE AWAKENING, Kate Chopin. 128pp. 27786-0 $1.00

THE RIME OF THE ANCIENT MARINER AND OTHER POEMS, Samuel Taylor Coleridge. 80pp. 27266-4 $1.00

HEART OF DARKNESS, Joseph Conrad. 80pp. 26464-5 $1.00

THE RED BADGE OF COURAGE, Stephen Crane. 112pp. 26465-3 $1.00

A CHRISTMAS CAROL, Charles Dickens. 80pp. 26865-9 $1.00

THE CRICKET ON THE HEARTH AND OTHER CHRISTMAS STORIES, Charles Dickens. 128pp. 28039-X $1.00

SELECTED POEMS, Emily Dickinson. 64pp. 26466-1 $1.00

SELECTED POEMS, John Donne. 96pp. 27788-7 $1.00

NOTES FROM THE UNDERGROUND, Fyodor Dostoyevsky. 96pp. 27053-X $1.00

SIX GREAT SHERLOCK HOLMES STORIES, Sir Arthur Conan Doyle. 112pp. 27055-6 $1.00

THE SOULS OF BLACK FOLK, W. E. B. Du Bois. 176pp. 28041-1 $2.00

MEDEA, Euripides. 64pp. 27548-5 $1.00

A BOY'S WILL AND NORTH OF BOSTON, Robert Frost. 112pp. (Available in U.S. only) 26866-7 $1.00

WHERE ANGELS FEAR TO TREAD, E. M. Forster. 128pp. (Available in U.S. only) 27791-7 $1.00

FAUST, PART ONE, Johann Wolfgang von Goethe. 192pp. 28046-2 $2.00

THE SCARLET LETTER, Nathaniel Hawthorne. 192pp. 28048-9 $2.00

A DOLL'S HOUSE, Henrik Ibsen. 80pp. 27062-9 $1.00

THE TURN OF THE SCREW, Henry James. 96pp. 26684-2 $1.00

VOLPONE, Ben Jonson. 112pp. 28049-7 $1.00

DUBLINERS, James Joyce. 160pp. 26870-5 $1.00

A PORTRAIT OF THE ARTIST AS A YOUNG MAN, James Joyce. 192pp. 28050-0 $2.00

LYRIC POEMS, John Keats. 80pp. 26871-3 $1.00

THE BOOK OF PSALMS, King James Bible. 144pp. 27541-8 $1.00